The Parable of the Sower

Christian fiction, Volume 8

Gregory Allen Parker

Published by Graywolf Press, 2024.

THE PARABLE OF THE SOWER

First edition. August 10, 2024.

Copyright © 2024 Gregory Allen Parker.

ISBN: 979-8227102584

Written by Gregory Allen Parker.

Table of Contents

To all those who seek to cultivate hearts open to God's transformative word, may this exploration of "The Parable of the Sower" guide you on your spiritual journey. To my family and friends, whose unwavering support and love have been the fertile ground in my life, nurturing and inspiring me daily. And to every reader, may you find the deep roots of faith, grow in wisdom, and bear abundant fruit for the Kingdom of Heaven.

Chapter 1: The Setting

Summary: Introduction to the setting where Jesus speaks to a large crowd by the sea.

    Bible Verse: Matthew 13:1-2

The sun had just risen over the horizon, casting its golden light across the Sea of Galilee. The waters shimmered, reflecting the morning glow, and the gentle breeze carried the scent of the sea mixed with the fragrances of blooming wildflowers along the shoreline. It was a peaceful and serene scene, yet it was about to become the setting for a profound and transformative event.

Jesus, the teacher from Nazareth, had become known throughout the region for His wisdom, compassion, and the miracles He performed. People from all walks of life were drawn to Him, seeking healing, hope, and the truth about the Kingdom of Heaven. On this particular morning, the crowd that gathered was larger than usual. News had spread quickly about His whereabouts, and a multitude of people had come to hear Him speak.

The crowd was a diverse tapestry of humanity. There were fishermen and farmers, merchants and laborers, the wealthy and the poor, the healthy and the sick. Each person had their own story, their own reason for being there. Some were curious, some were skeptical, and some were desperate for a touch of divine intervention. Among them were the disciples, close followers of Jesus who had left everything to walk with Him and learn from Him.

As the crowd grew, it became evident that there was no place large enough on land for everyone to gather comfortably. The people pressed in around Jesus, eager to be close to Him, to hear every word He spoke. Understanding the need for a better setting, Jesus devised a plan that would allow Him to address the multitude more effectively. He saw a small boat moored nearby and decided to use it as His pulpit.

Jesus turned to His disciples and instructed them to push the boat a little away from the shore. He stepped into the boat, and they did as He asked, creating a natural amphitheater with the water's edge as the stage. The people lined the shore, sitting on the soft grass and sandy beach, their eyes fixed on Jesus, waiting expectantly for His words.

The gentle lapping of the waves against the boat provided a soothing background sound, and the sea breeze carried Jesus' voice clearly to the crowd. The setting was perfect for the message He was about to deliver. It was here, in this picturesque scene, that Jesus chose to teach the people through parables—simple yet profound stories that revealed deep spiritual truths.

As He looked out over the crowd, Jesus saw the anticipation in their eyes. He knew their hearts, their struggles, and their hopes. He understood that the parables He would share needed to resonate with their everyday experiences while also challenging them to think more deeply about their lives and their relationship with God.

With a calm and steady voice, Jesus began to speak. "Behold, a sower went forth to sow," He said, and with these words, He set the stage for a parable that would illuminate the nature of the Kingdom of Heaven and the human heart's response to God's word.

The crowd listened intently as Jesus described the sower scattering seeds. Some seeds fell by the wayside, where birds quickly devoured them. Other seeds fell on stony ground, where they sprang up quickly but withered away under the scorching sun because they had no root. Some seeds fell among thorns, which grew up and choked the plants. But some seeds fell on good ground, producing a bountiful harvest.

As Jesus spoke, His words painted vivid images in the minds of His listeners. They could picture the sower walking through the fields, the seeds flying from his hand, and the different types of soil receiving the seeds. Yet, the parable's deeper meaning was not immediately apparent to everyone. It was a story that required reflection and insight to understand fully.

Jesus concluded the parable with a powerful exhortation: "He who has ears to hear, let him hear." These words challenged the listeners to go beyond the surface of the story and seek its spiritual significance. It was a call to openness, to a willingness to receive and embrace the truths of the Kingdom of Heaven.

After Jesus finished speaking, a hush fell over the crowd. The parable had sparked curiosity and contemplation. Some people began to discuss it among themselves, trying to decipher its meaning. Others remained silent, pondering the images and words they had just heard. The disciples, too, were intrigued and sought to understand the full depth of Jesus' teaching.

As the crowd slowly dispersed, many lingered by the shore, reluctant to leave the place where they had encountered such profound wisdom. The setting sun cast long shadows across the land, and the Sea of Galilee glowed with the warm hues of twilight. The day had been transformative, and the parable of the sower would continue to echo in the hearts and minds of those who had heard it.

For Jesus and His disciples, the day's teaching was far from over. As they returned to the shore and mingled with the crowd, people approached them with questions and requests for healing. Jesus, ever compassionate and patient, ministered to their needs, demonstrating the love and power of the Kingdom He proclaimed.

That evening, as the disciples gathered around Jesus, they asked Him to explain the parable in more detail. They wanted to understand its full significance and how it applied to their lives and ministry. Jesus, knowing their sincere desire for understanding, began to unfold the meaning of the parable to them.

He explained that the seed represented the word of God, and the different types of soil represented the various responses of people's hearts to that word. The wayside symbolized those who heard the word but did not understand it, allowing the evil one to snatch it away. The stony ground represented those who received the word with joy but fell away when troubles or persecution arose because they had no root. The thorns represented those who heard the word but allowed the worries of life and the deceitfulness of wealth to choke it, making it unfruitful. Finally, the good ground symbolized those who heard the word, understood it, and produced a fruitful harvest.

As Jesus spoke, the disciples' understanding deepened. They realized that the parable was not just a story about farming but a profound illustration of the spiritual realities they would encounter in their ministry. It highlighted the importance of the condition of one's heart in receiving and responding to God's word.

The disciples learned that their role as sowers of the word required patience, perseverance, and faith. They were called to scatter the seeds of the Kingdom widely, knowing that not every seed would bear fruit immediately. Some would be lost, others would face obstacles, but those that fell on good ground would yield a harvest beyond measure.

The setting by the sea had provided the perfect backdrop for this transformative teaching. It was a place where the natural beauty of God's creation met the profound truths of His Kingdom. As the disciples reflected on the day's events, they were filled with a renewed sense of purpose and dedication to their mission.

In the days and weeks that followed, the parable of the sower continued to be a central theme in Jesus' teachings. He used it as a foundation to build upon, sharing additional parables and teachings that further revealed the mysteries of the Kingdom of Heaven. The setting by the sea had been the starting point, a place where the seeds of truth were sown in the hearts of many, including the disciples.

As we reflect on this chapter, we are reminded of the timeless relevance of Jesus' teachings. The parable of the sower challenges us to examine the condition of our own hearts and our response to God's word. Are we like the wayside, the stony ground, or the thorns? Or are we like the good ground, ready to receive and nurture the word, allowing it to produce a fruitful harvest in our lives?

The setting by the Sea of Galilee serves as a powerful reminder that God's truth can be revealed in the most ordinary of places. It calls us to be attentive and receptive, to seek understanding and to apply the teachings of Jesus in our daily lives. Just as the disciples learned and grew from their time with Jesus, we too can grow in our faith and understanding, bearing fruit for the Kingdom of Heaven.

In conclusion, the setting of this chapter is not just a backdrop for a story but a profound illustration of the connection between the physical and the spiritual. It invites us to enter into the scene, to sit by the shore and listen to Jesus' words, and to allow those words to take root in our hearts, transforming us and leading us to a deeper understanding of the Kingdom of Heaven.

Chapter 2: The Sower

Summary: Introduction of the sower, symbolizing Jesus and His teachings.
Bible Verse: Matthew 13:3

The sun was just beginning to crest over the horizon, casting a golden glow over the fields that stretched out as far as the eye could see. The morning air was cool and crisp, carrying with it the fresh scent of dew-covered grass and blooming wildflowers. In the distance, the gentle hum of morning activity began as farmers prepared for another day of labor in the fields. It was a scene of peaceful industry, a testament to the rhythm of life that had sustained these people for generations.

Amid this serene landscape, a figure emerged, striding purposefully towards the fields with a sack slung over his shoulder. This was the sower, a man tasked with the vital work of planting seeds that would, in time, grow into a bountiful harvest. His steps were measured and deliberate, his demeanor one of quiet determination. As he approached the edge of the field, he paused for a moment, taking in the vast expanse of soil before him. With a practiced hand, he reached into his sack and began to scatter the seeds, each motion precise and purposeful.

The sower, as described in the parable told by Jesus, is a figure rich with symbolism. He represents not just the physical act of sowing seeds in a field, but also the spiritual act of spreading the word of God. In this parable, the sower symbolizes Jesus Himself, whose teachings were like seeds scattered upon the hearts of those who heard Him. Each seed held the potential to grow and bear fruit, depending on the condition of the soil in which it landed.

To understand the significance of the sower, it is essential to delve into the context of Jesus' ministry and the nature of His teachings. Jesus' message was revolutionary, challenging the established religious norms and offering a new understanding of God's Kingdom. He spoke of love, mercy, and justice, calling people to repentance and a deeper relationship with God. His teachings were not just for the religious elite but for all people, regardless of their social status or background.

As Jesus moved from town to town, teaching in synagogues, on hillsides, and by the sea, He encountered a diverse array of individuals. Some were eager to hear His message and followed Him wherever He went, while others were skeptical or outright hostile. The response to His teachings varied widely, much like the different types of soil described in the parable. Some hearts were receptive, ready to embrace the truth and allow it to transform their lives. Others were hardened or distracted, unable to grasp the deeper meaning of His words.

The parable of the sower is a powerful illustration of this dynamic. It highlights the importance of the sower's role in planting the seeds of truth, but it also emphasizes the responsibility of the hearers to receive and nurture those seeds. Jesus' teachings were meant to provoke thought, challenge assumptions, and inspire action. They were not merely words to be heard and forgotten but seeds to be planted, tended, and brought to fruition.

As the sower in the parable went forth to sow, he encountered different types of soil, each representing a different response to the word of God. The seeds that fell by the wayside were quickly eaten by birds, symbolizing those who hear the word but do not understand it, allowing the evil one to snatch it away. The seeds that fell on stony ground sprang up quickly but withered away under the scorching sun because they had no root, representing those who receive the word with joy but fall away when troubles or persecution arise. The seeds that fell among thorns were choked by the competing plants, symbolizing those who hear the word but allow the worries of life and the deceitfulness of wealth to choke it, making it unfruitful. Finally, the seeds that fell on good ground produced a bountiful harvest, representing those who hear the word, understand it, and bear fruit.

In exploring the role of the sower, it is crucial to recognize the qualities that make him effective. The sower is diligent, patient, and hopeful. He understands that not every seed will take root and grow, but he continues to sow because he believes in the potential of each seed. This perseverance and faith are essential for anyone tasked with sharing the message of the Kingdom of God. It requires a deep trust in the power of God's word and a commitment to the work of sowing, regardless of the immediate results.

The sower's task is also marked by a sense of purpose and intentionality. He does not scatter the seeds haphazardly but with a clear understanding of his mission. Each seed is an opportunity for growth, a chance to bring forth life and abundance. This sense of purpose is mirrored in Jesus' ministry. Every word He spoke, every parable He told, and every miracle He performed was done with the intent of revealing the Kingdom of Heaven and inviting people to enter into it. His actions were deliberate, guided by a profound love for humanity and a desire to see people transformed by the truth.

As the sower continues his work, he encounters the various types of soil that Jesus described in the parable. These soils represent the different conditions of the human heart and the varying responses to the word of God. The first type of soil, the wayside, is hard and unyielding. The seeds that fall here are quickly snatched away by birds, symbolizing the forces that prevent people from understanding and accepting the truth. This could be the result of spiritual blindness, hardened hearts, or distractions that keep people from truly hearing the message.

The second type of soil, the stony ground, offers a superficial response to the word. The seeds that fall here spring up quickly but wither away because they lack depth. This represents those who initially receive the word with enthusiasm but do not have a strong foundation. When challenges and persecutions come, their faith falters, and they fall away. This highlights the importance of a deep and rooted faith, one that can withstand the trials and tribulations of life.

The third type of soil, the thorny ground, is where the seeds are choked by competing plants. This symbolizes those who hear the word but are overwhelmed by the cares of this world and the deceitfulness of wealth. The distractions and temptations of life can suffocate the growth of the word, preventing it from bearing fruit. This serves as a warning about the dangers of allowing worldly concerns to dominate our hearts and minds.

Finally, the good ground represents those who hear the word, understand it, and allow it to take root in their hearts. These individuals produce a bountiful harvest, their lives reflecting the transformative power of the Kingdom of Heaven. This type of soil symbolizes a receptive and fertile heart, one that is open to God's truth and willing to be changed by it. It is a reminder that true spiritual growth requires a willingness to receive, nurture, and act upon the word of God.

The parable of the sower is not just a story about agriculture; it is a profound lesson about the nature of God's Kingdom and the human heart. It challenges us to examine the condition of our own hearts and consider how we respond to the word of God. Are we like the wayside, the stony ground, or the thorny ground, allowing distractions, difficulties, or hardness of heart to prevent us from truly embracing the truth? Or are we like the good ground, ready to receive the word and allow it to transform our lives?

In the context of Jesus' ministry, the parable of the sower serves as both an encouragement and a challenge. It encourages those who spread the word of God to persevere in their efforts, knowing that not every seed will bear fruit immediately, but the potential for a bountiful harvest exists. It challenges the hearers to examine their hearts and be receptive to the truth, allowing it to take root and grow.

As we reflect on the role of the sower, we are reminded of the importance of Jesus' teachings and the impact they can have on our lives. Jesus, as the ultimate sower, scattered the seeds of truth widely, offering hope, healing, and salvation to all who would receive it. His teachings continue to resonate across the centuries, challenging us to live lives that reflect the values of the Kingdom of Heaven.

The parable of the sower also invites us to consider our role in the ongoing work of spreading the word of God. Just as the sower in the parable went forth to sow, we too are called to share the message of the Kingdom with others. This requires diligence, patience, and faith, trusting that God will bring forth a harvest in His time. It also requires a deep commitment to nurturing our own spiritual growth, ensuring that our hearts are receptive to God's word and that we are living lives that bear fruit.

In conclusion, the parable of the sower is a powerful reminder of the transformative power of Jesus' teachings and the importance of our response to them. The sower, as a symbol of Jesus, represents the diligent, purposeful, and hopeful work of spreading the word of God. The different types of soil challenge us to examine our own hearts and consider how we receive and respond to the truth. As we continue to reflect on this parable, may we be inspired to cultivate hearts that are receptive to God's word and lives that bear fruit for the Kingdom of Heaven.

Chapter 3: The Seed by the Wayside

Summary: Description of the seeds that fell by the wayside and were eaten by birds.

Bible Verse: Matthew 13:4

As the sun ascended higher into the sky, its rays began to illuminate the landscape with a warm, golden light. The sower, whose story was unfolding in the parable told by Jesus, continued his task with steadfast dedication. His hand moved rhythmically, reaching into the sack slung over his shoulder to grasp handfuls of seeds, which he scattered across the field with practiced precision. Each seed, a potential bearer of life, was cast with hope and expectation.

In the parable, Jesus described the fate of some of these seeds with stark simplicity: "And as he sowed, some seeds fell by the wayside, and the birds came and devoured them" (Matthew 13:4). This vivid imagery paints a picture of seeds that, instead of finding fertile soil, land on the hardened, beaten path beside the field. Exposed and vulnerable, they are quickly snatched up by birds, their potential snuffed out before they even had a chance to sprout.

To fully grasp the significance of this part of the parable, it is essential to delve into the context and meaning behind the imagery Jesus used. The wayside represents a type of heart or mind that hears the word of God but does not understand or accept it. This lack of understanding leaves the seed, or the word, vulnerable to being taken away by the "birds," which symbolize the forces of evil or distraction that prevent the word from taking root.

The wayside, or the path, is a well-trodden area, compacted and hardened by the constant passage of people and animals. It is a place where seeds have little chance of penetrating the soil to begin their growth. This hardened ground symbolizes hearts that have been made resistant to God's word through various means—be it sin, pride, indifference, or the influence of worldly concerns. These are hearts that are not prepared to receive the message of the Kingdom, and as a result, the word does not penetrate but remains exposed and vulnerable.

In Jesus' time, the wayside paths would have been familiar sights to His audience. These were the routes that farmers and travelers used to move from place to place, often running alongside or through fields. The soil on these paths was compacted, resistant to the plow and the seed alike. When seeds fell upon these paths, they had no opportunity to sink into the earth and were easily picked off by birds.

The imagery of birds quickly swooping down to eat the seeds is striking. Birds, in this context, represent the forces of evil or distraction that seek to snatch away the word of God before it can take root. Just as the seeds are vulnerable on the hardened path, so too are the hearts and minds that do not understand or accept God's word. These forces can be likened to Satan and his efforts to prevent the word from taking effect in people's lives, as explained by Jesus in the interpretation of the parable found in Matthew 13:19: "When anyone hears the word of the kingdom and does not understand it, the evil one comes and snatches away what has been sown in his heart."

The condition of the wayside soil reflects a spiritual state of being closed off or resistant to God's truth. This resistance can arise from various factors. For some, it is a result of past hurts or disappointments that have hardened their hearts. For others, it may be pride or self-sufficiency that prevents them from seeing their need for God's guidance. Still, others may be so consumed with the cares and distractions of the world that they are unable to give proper attention to the spiritual truths being presented to them.

Consider the different ways in which people today can become like the wayside soil. In a world filled with constant noise and distraction, it is easy to see how the message of the Kingdom can be quickly drowned out. The rapid pace of modern life, with its relentless demands and diversions, can leave little room for contemplation and reflection. Many people live their lives on the surface, dealing only with immediate concerns and never delving deeper into the more profound questions of existence and purpose.

The media, technology, and various forms of entertainment can also contribute to this distraction. While these can be beneficial and enjoyable in moderation, they can also become overwhelming and all-consuming. When people's minds are constantly occupied with the latest news, social media updates, or the next big thing in entertainment, there is little room left for the quiet, introspective moments needed to engage with God's word.

Moreover, cultural and societal influences can play a significant role in shaping one's receptivity to the gospel. In many parts of the world, secularism and materialism dominate the cultural landscape, promoting values and priorities that are often at odds with the teachings of Jesus. The pursuit of wealth, success, and personal gratification can overshadow the pursuit of spiritual growth and understanding. This cultural milieu can create an environment where the word of God is not given the attention and reverence it deserves, leading to hearts that are hardened and unresponsive.

The wayside soil can also be seen in those who are indifferent or apathetic toward spiritual matters. These are individuals who, for various reasons, have no interest in seeking or understanding the deeper truths of life. They may view religion as irrelevant or outdated, something that has no bearing on their day-to-day existence. This indifference can be a significant barrier to receiving and understanding God's word, as it creates a mindset that is closed off to the transformative power of the gospel.

In contrast to the other types of soil described in the parable, the wayside offers a unique challenge to the sower. While the sower's efforts are consistent and diligent, the response of the wayside soil highlights the reality that not all hearts will be receptive to the message of the Kingdom. It underscores the importance of cultivating a receptive heart, one that is open to hearing and understanding God's word.

The parable of the sower, with its description of the seeds that fell by the wayside, calls us to examine our own hearts and minds. Are we like the wayside soil, hardened and resistant to God's truth? Do we allow distractions, pride, or indifference to prevent us from fully engaging with the message of the Kingdom? These are critical questions to consider as we seek to deepen our relationship with God and grow in our faith.

To avoid becoming like the wayside soil, it is essential to cultivate a heart that is receptive to God's word. This involves several key practices:

1. Cultivating Humility: Pride can be a significant barrier to receiving God's word. By cultivating humility and recognizing our need for God's guidance and wisdom, we open ourselves up to His truth. Humility allows us to approach God's word with a teachable spirit, ready to learn and grow.

2. Prioritizing Quiet Time: In a world filled with constant noise and distraction, it is crucial to set aside regular time for quiet reflection and

meditation on God's word. This time allows us to connect with God on a deeper level and create space for His truth to penetrate our hearts.

3. Engaging in Community: Surrounding ourselves with a community of believers can provide support and encouragement in our spiritual journey. Being part of a church or small group allows us to discuss and reflect on God's word together, gaining new insights and perspectives.

4. Seeking Understanding: Actively seeking to understand God's word involves studying the Bible, asking questions, and seeking guidance from trusted spiritual mentors. This intentional pursuit of understanding helps to prevent the word from being snatched away and allows it to take root in our hearts.

5. Guarding Against Distractions: Being mindful of the distractions that can divert our attention from God's word is essential. This may involve setting boundaries with technology, media, and other activities that can consume our time and focus.

6. Praying for Receptivity: Praying for a receptive heart and asking God to remove any barriers that prevent us from fully engaging with His word is a powerful practice. Prayer opens the door for the Holy Spirit to work in our lives, softening our hearts and making them more receptive to God's truth.

As we consider these practices, it is important to remember that the process of cultivating a receptive heart is ongoing. It requires consistent effort and a willingness to be transformed by God's word. The parable of the sower serves as a reminder of the potential for growth and transformation when we allow God's word to take root in our hearts.

The seeds that fell by the wayside may have been devoured by birds, but the parable does not end there. Jesus goes on to describe other types of soil that receive the seeds and produce varying degrees of harvest. This progression highlights the hope and possibility for fruitful growth when the word is received with understanding and nurtured with care.

In reflecting on the seeds that fell by the wayside, we are reminded of the importance of preparing our hearts to receive God's word. Just as a farmer prepares the soil before planting, we too must prepare our hearts through humility, quiet reflection, community engagement, and intentional study. By doing so, we create an environment where the word of God can take root, grow, and produce a bountiful harvest in our lives.

The parable of the sower, with its description of the seeds that fell by the wayside, challenges us to examine the condition of our own hearts and to take steps to ensure that we are receptive to God's truth. It calls us to cultivate a heart that is open, humble, and ready to receive the transformative power of the gospel. In doing so, we can experience the fullness of God's Kingdom and bear fruit that reflects His love, grace, and truth in our lives.

As we continue to explore the parable of the sower, let us be mindful of the lessons it teaches us about the different responses to God's word. Let us strive to be like the good soil, ready to receive, understand, and nurture the seeds of truth that are sown in our hearts. By doing so, we can experience the abundant life that Jesus promised and contribute to the growth of His Kingdom here on earth.

In conclusion, the seeds that fell by the wayside serve as a powerful reminder of the challenges and obstacles that can prevent the word of God from taking root in our hearts. However, they also highlight the importance of cultivating a receptive heart, one that is open to hearing, understanding, and embracing God's truth. As we reflect on this part of the parable, let us be inspired to take intentional steps to prepare our hearts to receive the word of God and to nurture it so that it can grow and bear fruit in our lives.

Chapter 4: The Seed on Stony Ground

Summary: Description of the seeds that fell on stony ground and withered away because they had no root.
Bible Verse: Matthew 13:5-6

The morning sun continued its ascent, casting long shadows across the fields and illuminating the varied terrain that the sower navigated with his bag of seeds. The air was filled with the sounds of nature awakening—a symphony of birds chirping, insects buzzing, and the rustling of leaves in the gentle breeze. It was amidst this setting that the sower's diligent work proceeded, his hands rhythmically scattering seeds across the land, each one a potential bearer of new life and growth.

As Jesus recounted in His parable, some of these seeds fell on stony ground: "Some fell upon stony places, where they had not much earth: and forthwith they sprung up, because they had no deepness of earth: And when the sun was up, they were scorched; and because they had no root, they withered away" (Matthew 13:5-6). This vivid illustration of seeds landing on rocky soil provides a profound insight into the nature of spiritual receptivity and the challenges that can arise in the journey of faith.

To fully appreciate the significance of this part of the parable, it is essential to explore the characteristics of stony ground and the implications for the seeds that fall upon it. Stony ground, unlike the fertile soil, presents a harsh and inhospitable environment for seeds. The thin layer of soil covering the rocks may initially appear suitable for planting, but it lacks the depth needed for roots to grow and anchor the plant. As a result, seeds that fall on stony ground may germinate quickly but are ultimately doomed to wither and die under the harsh conditions.

The stony ground symbolizes a type of heart that is initially receptive to the word of God but lacks the depth and foundation necessary for sustained spiritual growth. This superficial acceptance is often characterized by enthusiasm and excitement, but it is not accompanied by a deep and abiding commitment. When challenges and difficulties arise, this shallow faith quickly falters, unable to withstand the pressures of life.

In Jesus' time, stony ground would have been a familiar sight to His listeners. The rocky terrain of the region made farming a challenging endeavor, requiring careful preparation and cultivation to ensure that seeds could take root and thrive. The imagery of seeds springing up quickly on stony ground but withering away under the scorching sun would have resonated with the agricultural experience of His audience.

The seeds that fall on stony ground represent those who hear the word of God and initially receive it with joy and enthusiasm. These individuals may experience an emotional response to the message, feeling inspired and motivated to embrace the teachings of Jesus. However, their faith remains shallow, lacking the deep roots needed to sustain it through the trials and tribulations of life.

This superficial faith is vulnerable to the scorching heat of adversity. When faced with difficulties, such as persecution, suffering, or personal challenges, these individuals find that their shallow roots provide no support. Without a strong foundation, their faith withers, and they fall away from their initial commitment. The enthusiasm and joy that once characterized their response to the word of God are quickly replaced by doubt, fear, and disillusionment.

To understand why some hearts are like stony ground, it is important to consider the various factors that can contribute to a superficial faith. One such factor is the allure of emotional experiences without a corresponding depth of understanding. In today's world, it is not uncommon for people to be drawn to charismatic speakers, emotional worship services, or powerful testimonies. While these experiences can be valuable and inspiring, they must be accompanied by a commitment to deeper spiritual growth and understanding.

Another factor contributing to superficial faith is a lack of intentional discipleship and mentorship. New believers, or those who are returning to their faith after a period of absence, may not receive the guidance and support needed to develop a strong and resilient faith. Without proper discipleship, their initial enthusiasm may fade, leaving them vulnerable to the challenges and doubts that inevitably arise.

Additionally, cultural and societal pressures can play a significant role in shaping the depth of one's faith. In many parts of the world, the pursuit of material success, social status, and personal gratification can overshadow the pursuit of spiritual growth. When the values and priorities of the culture conflict with the teachings of Jesus, individuals may find it difficult to maintain a deep and abiding commitment to their faith.

The stony ground also represents the presence of unresolved issues or hidden obstacles within one's heart. Just as rocks beneath the surface of the soil can impede the growth of a plant, unresolved emotional wounds, unconfessed sins, and lingering doubts can hinder the development of a strong and resilient faith. These hidden obstacles must be addressed and removed to allow for deep spiritual growth.

To avoid becoming like the stony ground, it is essential to cultivate a faith that is both deep and resilient. This involves several key practices:

1. Commitment to Discipleship: Intentional discipleship is crucial for developing a strong and resilient faith. This includes regular study of the Bible, participation in a faith community, and seeking guidance from mature believers who can provide support and mentorship.

2. Deepening Understanding: A deep and abiding faith requires a commitment to understanding the teachings of Jesus and applying them to one's life. This involves not only reading the Bible but also engaging with it through prayer, meditation, and study. Seeking to understand the historical and cultural context of the scriptures can also provide valuable insights.

3. Developing Resilience: Building a resilient faith involves preparing for the inevitable challenges and difficulties that will arise. This includes developing a strong prayer life, cultivating spiritual disciplines such as fasting and solitude, and learning to trust in God's faithfulness even in the face of adversity.

4. Addressing Hidden Obstacles: Unresolved emotional wounds, unconfessed sins, and lingering doubts can hinder spiritual growth. It is important to address these issues through prayer, confession, and seeking counsel from trusted spiritual advisors. Removing these hidden obstacles allows for deeper roots to grow and strengthen one's faith.

5. Balancing Emotion with Depth: While emotional experiences can be valuable and inspiring, they must be balanced with a commitment to deeper

spiritual growth. This involves recognizing the limitations of emotional responses and seeking to develop a faith that is grounded in understanding and commitment.

6. Cultivating a Supportive Community: Surrounding oneself with a community of believers who provide support, encouragement, and accountability is essential for deepening one's faith. This community can help to sustain and nurture one's spiritual growth, providing a strong foundation in times of difficulty.

As we reflect on the seeds that fell on stony ground, we are reminded of the importance of cultivating a faith that is deep and resilient. Superficial enthusiasm is not enough to sustain us through the trials and tribulations of life. We must be intentional in our pursuit of spiritual growth, seeking to develop a strong foundation that can withstand the pressures and challenges that will inevitably come.

The parable of the sower, with its description of the seeds that fell on stony ground, challenges us to examine the depth of our own faith. Are we like the stony ground, with a superficial faith that withers under pressure? Or are we committed to developing a deep and resilient faith that can endure the trials of life? These are critical questions to consider as we seek to grow in our relationship with God and live out the teachings of Jesus.

The imagery of seeds withering on stony ground serves as a powerful reminder of the potential consequences of a shallow faith. Just as the scorching sun can cause unrooted plants to wither and die, the trials and challenges of life can cause superficial faith to falter. This underscores the importance of developing a faith that is deeply rooted in God's word and capable of withstanding adversity.

In exploring the characteristics of stony ground, we are also called to consider how we can support others in their spiritual journey. Just as the sower continues to scatter seeds despite the presence of stony ground, we too are called to share the message of the Kingdom with those around us. This involves providing support, encouragement, and guidance to help others develop a deep and resilient faith.

Supporting others in their spiritual journey requires a commitment to intentional discipleship and mentorship. This includes walking alongside new believers, providing guidance and support as they navigate the challenges of faith. It also involves creating an environment where questions and doubts can be openly discussed and addressed, allowing for deeper understanding and growth.

As we consider the role of the sower and the challenges posed by stony ground, we are reminded of the importance of perseverance in our efforts to share the message of the Kingdom. Not every seed will take root and grow, but the potential for a bountiful harvest exists when we remain faithful to our calling. This perseverance requires a deep trust in God's faithfulness and a commitment to the work of sowing, regardless of the immediate results.

The parable of the sower, with its description of the seeds that fell on stony ground, invites us to reflect on our own faith journey and the ways in which we can cultivate a deep and resilient faith. It challenges us to examine the obstacles and hidden issues that may hinder our spiritual growth and to take intentional steps to address them. It also calls us to support others in their journey, providing the guidance and encouragement needed to develop a strong foundation in their faith.

In conclusion, the seeds that fell on stony ground serve as a powerful reminder of the importance of developing a faith that is deep and resilient. Superficial enthusiasm is not enough to sustain us through the trials and challenges of life. We must be intentional in our pursuit of spiritual growth, seeking to develop a strong foundation that can withstand the pressures and difficulties that will inevitably come. As we reflect on this part of the parable, may we be inspired to cultivate a faith that is deeply rooted in God's word and capable of bearing fruit for His Kingdom.

Chapter 5: The Seed Among Thorns

Summary: Description of the seeds that fell among thorns and were choked.

Bible Verse: Matthew 13:7

The morning sun, now high in the sky, bathed the fields in a bright, warm light. The sower continued his task, his hands moving steadily as he scattered seeds across the varied landscape. Each seed held the promise of life, a potential harvest that could provide sustenance and nourishment. But not all seeds would fulfill this promise. Some would face obstacles that would hinder their growth and prevent them from reaching their full potential.

As Jesus explained in His parable, some of the seeds fell among thorns: "And some fell among thorns; and the thorns sprung up, and choked them" (Matthew 13:7). This vivid imagery paints a picture of seeds that initially begin to grow but are soon overwhelmed and suffocated by the surrounding thorns. To fully grasp the significance of this part of the parable, it is essential to explore the nature of the thorns and the impact they have on the growth of the seeds.

Thorns, with their sharp, invasive nature, symbolize the various distractions and temptations that can divert our attention from spiritual growth and choke out the word of God. These distractions can take many forms, such as the pursuit of wealth, the desire for material possessions, the worries of everyday life, and the allure of worldly pleasures. The thorns represent anything that competes with and ultimately stifles our commitment to following Jesus and living according to His teachings.

In the context of the parable, the thorns are a powerful metaphor for the spiritual dangers that can entangle and suffocate our faith. Just as thorns can crowd out and overshadow young plants, preventing them from receiving the sunlight and nutrients they need to thrive, so too can the cares and distractions of life crowd out our devotion to God. The seeds that fall among thorns may initially show signs of growth, but they are eventually overwhelmed and choked, unable to bear fruit.

To understand why some hearts are like the thorny ground, it is important to consider the various factors that contribute to this spiritual condition. One such factor is the pervasive influence of materialism and consumerism in today's world. The relentless pursuit of wealth and possessions can consume our thoughts and energies, leaving little room for spiritual reflection and growth. The desire for more—more money, more status, more things—can become an all-encompassing focus that chokes out our commitment to God's word.

Another factor is the constant barrage of information and stimuli that characterizes modern life. With the advent of technology and the internet, we are bombarded with news, advertisements, social media updates, and countless other distractions. This constant influx of information can overwhelm our minds and make it difficult to maintain a clear and focused relationship with God. The noise and busyness of life can drown out the still, small voice of the Holy Spirit, preventing us from hearing and responding to God's word.

The worries and anxieties of life can also act as thorns that choke our faith. Concerns about health, finances, relationships, and the future can dominate our thoughts and sap our spiritual vitality. When we are consumed by worry, we become like the seed among thorns, our faith stifled by the cares of this world. Jesus addressed this issue directly in His teachings, reminding His followers not to be anxious about their lives but to trust in God's provision and care (Matthew 6:25-34).

Additionally, the allure of worldly pleasures and sinful desires can act as thorns that choke our spiritual growth. The temptation to indulge in behaviors and activities that are contrary to God's will can lead us away from a life of holiness and devotion. These temptations can be subtle and insidious, gradually drawing us away from our commitment to Christ and entangling us in sin. The pursuit of pleasure, whether through substance abuse, sexual immorality, or other forms of self-gratification, can choke out the word of God and prevent us from bearing fruit.

In light of these challenges, it is essential to take intentional steps to prevent the thorns of life from choking our faith. This involves several key practices:

1. Cultivating Contentment: The pursuit of material wealth and possessions can be a significant distraction from spiritual growth. Cultivating a spirit of contentment and gratitude can help us focus on what truly matters and prevent the thorns of materialism from taking root in our hearts. This involves recognizing the sufficiency of God's provision and finding joy in the blessings we already have.

2. Simplifying Our Lives: The constant barrage of information and stimuli can overwhelm our minds and make it difficult to maintain a clear and focused

relationship with God. Simplifying our lives by reducing unnecessary distractions and creating space for quiet reflection and prayer can help us stay connected to God's word. This may involve setting boundaries with technology, practicing mindfulness, and prioritizing time for spiritual disciplines.

3. Trusting in God's Provision: Worries and anxieties can choke our faith and prevent us from experiencing the fullness of God's peace. Learning to trust in God's provision and care involves surrendering our concerns to Him and relying on His faithfulness. This trust is cultivated through prayer, meditation on God's promises, and seeking support from a faith community.

4. Resisting Temptation: The allure of worldly pleasures and sinful desires can entangle us and choke our spiritual growth. Resisting temptation requires a commitment to holiness and a reliance on the power of the Holy Spirit. This involves being vigilant against the subtle and insidious nature of temptation, seeking accountability from fellow believers, and immersing ourselves in God's word.

5. Prioritizing Spiritual Growth: To prevent the thorns of life from choking our faith, it is essential to prioritize spiritual growth and make it a central focus of our lives. This involves regular engagement with the Bible, prayer, worship, and fellowship with other believers. By keeping our eyes fixed on Jesus and seeking to grow in our relationship with Him, we can ensure that our faith remains strong and vibrant.

As we reflect on the seeds that fell among thorns, we are reminded of the importance of cultivating a heart that is free from the distractions and entanglements of this world. The thorns represent the various obstacles that can hinder our spiritual growth and prevent us from bearing fruit. To avoid becoming like the thorny ground, we must be intentional in our efforts to remove these obstacles and create an environment where God's word can flourish.

The parable of the sower, with its description of the seeds that fell among thorns, challenges us to examine the priorities and distractions in our own lives. Are we allowing the cares and temptations of this world to choke our faith? Are we so consumed with the pursuit of material wealth, social status, and personal pleasure that we neglect our relationship with God? These are critical questions to consider as we seek to live out the teachings of Jesus and grow in our faith.

The imagery of seeds being choked by thorns serves as a powerful reminder of the potential consequences of allowing worldly distractions to dominate our lives. Just as thorns can suffocate young plants, preventing them from receiving the sunlight and nutrients they need to thrive, so too can the cares and temptations of life suffocate our spiritual growth. This underscores the importance of being vigilant and intentional in our efforts to cultivate a heart that is receptive to God's word.

In exploring the characteristics of thorny ground, we are also called to consider how we can support others in their spiritual journey. Just as the sower continues to scatter seeds despite the presence of thorns, we too are called to share the message of the Kingdom with those around us. This involves providing support, encouragement, and guidance to help others navigate the distractions and temptations that can hinder their faith.

Supporting others in their spiritual journey requires a commitment to intentional discipleship and mentorship. This includes walking alongside new believers, providing guidance and support as they navigate the challenges of faith. It also involves creating an environment where questions and doubts can be openly discussed and addressed, allowing for deeper understanding and growth.

As we consider the role of the sower and the challenges posed by thorny ground, we are reminded of the importance of perseverance in our efforts to share the message of the Kingdom. Not every seed will take root and grow, but the potential for a bountiful harvest exists when we remain faithful to our calling. This perseverance requires a deep trust in God's faithfulness and a commitment to the work of sowing, regardless of the immediate results.

The parable of the sower, with its description of the seeds that fell among thorns, invites us to reflect on our own faith journey and the ways in which we can cultivate a heart that is free from the distractions and entanglements of this world. It challenges us to examine the obstacles and hidden issues that may hinder our spiritual growth and to take intentional steps to address them. It also calls us to support others in their journey, providing the guidance and encouragement needed to develop a strong foundation in their faith.

In conclusion, the seeds that fell among thorns serve as a powerful reminder of the importance of cultivating a heart that is free from the distractions and entanglements of this world. The thorns represent the various obstacles that can hinder our spiritual growth and prevent us from bearing fruit. To avoid becoming like the thorny ground, we must be intentional in our efforts to remove these obstacles and create an environment where God's word can flourish. As we reflect on this part of the parable, may we be inspired to cultivate a heart that is receptive to God's word and capable of bearing fruit for His Kingdom.

Chapter 6: The Seed on Good Ground

Summary: Description of the seeds that fell on good ground and brought forth fruit.

Bible Verse: Matthew 13:8

The day had grown warmer as the sun reached its zenith, casting a brilliant light over the fields where the sower continued his work. His hands moved with a practiced rhythm, scattering seeds with hope and purpose. Each seed carried within it the potential for life and abundance, and the sower's heart was filled with the anticipation of the harvest to come. It was in this moment, as he sowed his seeds, that Jesus' parable reached its climax with the description of the seeds that fell on good ground: "But other fell into good ground, and brought forth fruit, some an hundredfold, some sixtyfold, some thirtyfold" (Matthew 13:8).

This part of the parable provides a profound and hopeful image of spiritual growth and fruitfulness. Unlike the seeds that fell by the wayside, on stony ground, or among thorns, the seeds that landed on good ground found a receptive and fertile environment. These seeds not only took root but also flourished, producing a bountiful harvest that far exceeded expectations. To fully appreciate the significance of this good ground, it is essential to explore its characteristics, the process of cultivation, and the implications for our spiritual lives.

Good ground, in the context of the parable, represents a heart that is open, receptive, and prepared to receive the word of God. It is a heart that is free from the hardness of the wayside, the shallowness of stony ground, and the distractions of thorns. This fertile soil provides the ideal conditions for seeds to take root, grow, and bear fruit. The image of a bountiful harvest—some a hundredfold, some sixtyfold, some thirtyfold—highlights the transformative power of God's word when it is received with faith and nurtured with care.

To understand what makes ground "good" in a spiritual sense, we must consider several key characteristics:

1. Openness and Receptivity: Good ground is characterized by an openness to God's word. This means having a heart that is willing to listen, learn, and be

transformed by the teachings of Jesus. Openness involves a readiness to receive the truth, even when it challenges our preconceived notions or requires us to change our ways.

2. Depth and Understanding: Unlike the shallow soil of stony ground, good ground provides depth for roots to grow and anchor the plant. In a spiritual context, this depth represents a thorough understanding of God's word and a commitment to applying it in our lives. It involves studying the scriptures, seeking wisdom, and cultivating a deep relationship with God.

3. Freedom from Distractions: Good ground is free from the competing plants and weeds that can choke the growth of seeds. Spiritually, this means being free from the distractions and temptations of the world that can divert our attention from God's word. It involves prioritizing our relationship with God and being vigilant against the things that can pull us away from Him.

4. Fertility and Nourishment: Good ground is fertile and provides the necessary nutrients for seeds to grow. This represents a heart that is nourished by prayer, worship, fellowship, and other spiritual disciplines. It involves creating an environment where God's word can thrive and produce fruit.

Cultivating good ground in our hearts requires intentional effort and commitment. Just as a farmer prepares the soil to ensure a successful harvest, we must prepare our hearts to receive and nurture God's word. This involves several key practices:

1. Prayer and Reflection: Regular prayer and reflection help to keep our hearts open and receptive to God's word. Through prayer, we invite the Holy Spirit to work in our lives, softening our hearts and making them fertile ground for spiritual growth.

2. Study and Meditation: Engaging with the scriptures through study and meditation deepens our understanding of God's word. This involves not only reading the Bible but also reflecting on its meaning, seeking to understand its context, and applying its teachings to our lives.

3. Repentance and Renewal: Cultivating good ground requires a willingness to repent of our sins and seek God's forgiveness. Repentance involves turning away from the things that hinder our spiritual growth and seeking to renew our commitment to following Jesus.

4. Community and Fellowship: Being part of a faith community provides support, encouragement, and accountability in our spiritual journey.

Fellowship with other believers helps to nourish our faith and provides opportunities for growth and service.

5. Service and Mission: Actively serving others and participating in God's mission helps to cultivate a heart that is focused on bearing fruit for the Kingdom. Service involves using our gifts and talents to bless others and advance God's purposes in the world.

As we consider the image of good ground, we are reminded of the potential for spiritual fruitfulness when we receive and nurture God's word. The seeds that fell on good ground produced a bountiful harvest, reflecting the abundant life that Jesus promised to those who follow Him. This fruitfulness is not just for our benefit but also for the benefit of others and the glory of God.

The parable of the sower, with its description of the seeds that fell on good ground, challenges us to examine the condition of our own hearts. Are we open and receptive to God's word? Are we committed to understanding and applying its teachings in our lives? Are we free from the distractions and temptations that can choke our faith? These are important questions to consider as we seek to cultivate good ground in our hearts and experience the transformative power of God's word.

The imagery of a bountiful harvest also invites us to reflect on the impact of our spiritual growth on others. Just as a farmer's harvest provides food and sustenance for many, our spiritual fruitfulness can bless those around us. When we bear fruit for the Kingdom, we become channels of God's love, grace, and truth, making a positive difference in the lives of others.

In exploring the characteristics of good ground, we are also called to consider how we can support others in their spiritual journey. Just as the sower scatters seeds with hope and purpose, we too are called to share the message of the Kingdom with those around us. This involves providing support, encouragement, and guidance to help others cultivate good ground in their hearts and experience the transformative power of God's word.

Supporting others in their spiritual journey requires a commitment to intentional discipleship and mentorship. This includes walking alongside new believers, providing guidance and support as they navigate the challenges of faith. It also involves creating an environment where questions and doubts can be openly discussed and addressed, allowing for deeper understanding and growth.

As we consider the role of the sower and the potential for a bountiful harvest on good ground, we are reminded of the importance of perseverance in our efforts to share the message of the Kingdom. Not every seed will take root and grow, but the potential for a bountiful harvest exists when we remain faithful to our calling. This perseverance requires a deep trust in God's faithfulness and a commitment to the work of sowing, regardless of the immediate results.

The parable of the sower, with its description of the seeds that fell on good ground, invites us to reflect on our own faith journey and the ways in which we can cultivate a heart that is open, receptive, and prepared to receive God's word. It challenges us to examine the obstacles and hidden issues that may hinder our spiritual growth and to take intentional steps to address them. It also calls us to support others in their journey, providing the guidance and encouragement needed to develop a strong foundation in their faith.

In conclusion, the seeds that fell on good ground serve as a powerful reminder of the potential for spiritual growth and fruitfulness when we receive and nurture God's word. The good ground represents a heart that is open, receptive, and prepared to receive the truth of the Kingdom. To cultivate such a heart, we must be intentional in our efforts to engage with God's word, prioritize our spiritual growth, and remove the obstacles that hinder our faith. As we reflect on this part of the parable, may we be inspired to cultivate good ground in our hearts and bear fruit for God's Kingdom.

The Characteristics of Good Ground

Good ground, as described in Jesus' parable, is rich, fertile, and well-prepared to receive and nurture seeds. Spiritually, this good ground symbolizes a heart that is open, receptive, and eager to embrace the teachings of Jesus. To fully understand what makes ground "good," we need to explore several key characteristics:

1. Openness and Receptivity: A heart that is open to God's word is ready to listen, learn, and be transformed. This openness involves a willingness to hear the truth, even when it challenges our existing beliefs or requires us to change our behavior. It means being teachable and humble, recognizing that we do not have all the answers and that we need God's guidance.

2. Depth and Understanding: Good ground provides the necessary depth for roots to grow and anchor the plant. In a spiritual sense, this depth represents a thorough understanding of God's word and a commitment to applying it in our lives. It involves studying the scriptures, seeking wisdom, and cultivating a deep relationship with God. A shallow understanding of God's word is insufficient for sustained spiritual growth; we need to delve deeply into the teachings of Jesus and allow them to shape our lives.

3. Freedom from Distractions: Good ground is free from the competing plants and weeds that can choke the growth of seeds. Spiritually, this means being free from the distractions and temptations of the world that can divert our attention from God's word. It involves prioritizing our relationship with God and being vigilant against the things that can pull us away from Him. This requires discernment and intentionality in how we spend our time and energy.

4. Fertility and Nourishment: Good ground is fertile and provides the necessary nutrients for seeds to grow. This represents a heart that is nourished by prayer, worship, fellowship, and other spiritual disciplines. It involves creating an environment where God's word can thrive and produce fruit. Just as a plant needs water, sunlight, and nutrients to grow, our faith needs to be nourished by regular engagement with God and His community.

Cultivating good ground in our hearts requires intentional effort and commitment. Just as a farmer prepares the soil to ensure a successful harvest, we must prepare our hearts to receive and nurture God's word. This involves several key practices:

1. Prayer and Reflection: Regular prayer and reflection help to keep our hearts open and receptive to God's word. Through prayer, we invite the Holy Spirit to work in our lives, softening our hearts and making them fertile ground for spiritual growth. Reflection allows us to examine our lives in light of God's word and to make necessary adjustments.

2. Study and Meditation: Engaging with the scriptures through study and meditation deepens our understanding of God's word. This involves not only reading the Bible but also reflecting on its meaning, seeking to understand its context, and applying its teachings to our lives. Meditation on God's word helps to internalize its truths and allows them to shape our thoughts and actions.

3. Repentance and Renewal: Cultivating good ground requires a willingness to repent of our sins and seek God's forgiveness. Repentance involves turning away from the things that hinder our spiritual growth and seeking to renew our commitment to following Jesus. This process of repentance and renewal is ongoing, as we continually seek to align our lives with God's will.

4. Community and Fellowship: Being part of a faith community provides support, encouragement, and accountability in our spiritual journey. Fellowship with other believers helps to nourish our faith and provides opportunities for growth and service. In community, we can share our struggles, celebrate our victories, and support one another in our walk with God.

5. Service and Mission: Actively serving others and participating in God's mission helps to cultivate a heart that is focused on bearing fruit for the Kingdom. Service involves using our gifts and talents to bless others and advance God's purposes in the world. When we serve others, we reflect the love of Christ and demonstrate the transformative power of the gospel.

The Potential for a Bountiful Harvest

The image of a bountiful harvest—some a hundredfold, some sixtyfold, some thirtyfold—highlights the transformative power of God's word when it is received with faith and nurtured with care. The seeds that fell on good ground produced a harvest far beyond what could be expected, reflecting the abundant life that Jesus promised to those who follow Him. This fruitfulness is not just for our benefit but also for the benefit of others and the glory of God.

To understand the potential for a bountiful harvest, it is important to recognize that spiritual growth and fruitfulness are the result of God's work in our lives. While we have a role to play in cultivating good ground, it is ultimately God who gives the increase. The apostle Paul expressed this truth in his letter to the Corinthians: "I planted, Apollos watered, but God gave the growth. So neither the one who plants nor the one who waters is anything, but only God who gives the growth" (1 Corinthians 3:6-7). This recognition of God's sovereignty should inspire humility and dependence on Him as we seek to bear fruit for His Kingdom.

The bountiful harvest described in the parable also invites us to consider the various ways in which spiritual fruit can manifest in our lives. Spiritual fruit encompasses a wide range of expressions, including the development of Christlike character, the impact of our witness and testimony, and the influence of our service and ministry. Each of these areas reflects the transformative power of God's word and the work of the Holy Spirit in our lives.

1. Christlike Character: One of the most significant ways in which spiritual fruit can manifest is through the development of Christlike character. The apostle Paul described the "fruit of the Spirit" as qualities such as love, joy, peace, patience, kindness, goodness, faithfulness, gentleness, and self-control (Galatians 5:22-23). These characteristics reflect the nature of Christ and are evidence of His work in our lives. As we grow in our relationship with God, the Holy Spirit transforms us, producing these qualities in increasing measure.

2. Witness and Testimony: Another way in which spiritual fruit can manifest is through the impact of our witness and testimony. As followers of Jesus, we are called to be His witnesses, sharing the good news of the gospel with others. When we bear witness to the transforming power of God's word in our lives, we have the potential to influence others and draw them to Christ. Our testimony of God's faithfulness, grace, and love can inspire and encourage those around us, leading to spiritual growth and transformation in their lives as well.

3. Service and Ministry: Spiritual fruit can also manifest through our service and ministry to others. When we use our gifts and talents to bless and serve those around us, we reflect the love of Christ and advance God's purposes in the world. This service can take many forms, from acts of kindness and compassion to leadership and teaching roles within the church. The impact of our service extends beyond the immediate recipients, as it contributes to the overall growth and health of the body of Christ.

4. Influence and Legacy: The fruitfulness of our lives can have a lasting influence and legacy that extends beyond our lifetime. The seeds we plant through our words, actions, and relationships can continue to bear fruit in the lives of others long after we are gone. This enduring impact is a testament to the power of God's word and the work of the Holy Spirit in and through us. It is a reminder that our faithfulness in cultivating good ground can have a far-reaching and lasting effect.

Supporting Others in Their Spiritual Journey

In exploring the characteristics of good ground and the potential for a bountiful harvest, we are also called to consider how we can support others in their spiritual journey. Just as the sower scatters seeds with hope and purpose, we too are called to share the message of the Kingdom with those around us. This involves providing support, encouragement, and guidance to help others cultivate good ground in their hearts and experience the transformative power of God's word.

Supporting others in their spiritual journey requires a commitment to intentional discipleship and mentorship. This includes walking alongside new believers, providing guidance and support as they navigate the challenges of faith. It also involves creating an environment where questions and doubts can be openly discussed and addressed, allowing for deeper understanding and growth.

1. Discipleship and Mentorship: Intentional discipleship involves investing time and energy in the spiritual growth of others. This can take the form of one-on-one mentoring relationships, small group studies, or formal discipleship programs within the church. The goal of discipleship is to help others grow in their understanding of God's word, develop Christlike character, and become effective witnesses for the Kingdom.

2. Creating a Supportive Environment: A supportive environment is essential for spiritual growth. This includes fostering a culture of openness and authenticity within the church, where individuals feel safe to share their struggles and questions. It also involves providing resources and opportunities for growth, such as Bible studies, prayer groups, and service opportunities.

3. Encouragement and Accountability: Encouragement and accountability are vital components of supporting others in their spiritual journey. Encouragement involves affirming the progress and growth we see in others, as well as offering words of hope and comfort in times of difficulty. Accountability involves holding one another responsible for our commitments to follow Christ, helping each other stay on track and grow in our faith.

4. Prayer and Intercession: Praying for others is a powerful way to support their spiritual growth. Interceding on behalf of others involves lifting them up in prayer, asking God to work in their lives and to help them overcome

the obstacles they face. Prayer creates a spiritual bond and demonstrates our commitment to supporting one another in the journey of faith.

Perseverance in the Work of Sowing

As we consider the role of the sower and the potential for a bountiful harvest on good ground, we are reminded of the importance of perseverance in our efforts to share the message of the Kingdom. Not every seed will take root and grow, but the potential for a bountiful harvest exists when we remain faithful to our calling. This perseverance requires a deep trust in God's faithfulness and a commitment to the work of sowing, regardless of the immediate results.

The parable of the sower teaches us that the outcome of our efforts is ultimately in God's hands. While we are responsible for sowing the seeds and cultivating good ground, it is God who gives the increase. This recognition should inspire us to continue sowing with hope and faith, knowing that God can bring about a bountiful harvest in His time and according to His purposes.

Trusting in God's Timing: Spiritual growth and fruitfulness often take time. Just as a farmer waits patiently for the harvest, we must trust in God's timing and remain faithful in our efforts. There may be seasons of apparent inactivity or slow growth, but we can trust that God is at work, even when we do not see immediate results.

Staying Faithful in the Work: The work of sowing and cultivating good ground requires consistency and perseverance. This involves staying faithful in our spiritual disciplines, continuing to share the message of the Kingdom, and supporting others in their journey. Our faithfulness in these efforts is an expression of our trust in God's faithfulness.

Celebrating the Harvest: When we do see the fruit of our efforts, it is important to celebrate and give thanks to God. Celebrating the harvest reminds us of God's goodness and encourages us to continue in the work of sowing. It also provides an opportunity to share testimonies of God's faithfulness and to inspire others in their spiritual journey.

Conclusion

The seeds that fell on good ground serve as a powerful reminder of the potential for spiritual growth and fruitfulness when we receive and nurture God's word. The good ground represents a heart that is open, receptive, and prepared to receive the truth of the Kingdom. To cultivate such a heart, we must be intentional in our efforts to engage with God's word, prioritize our spiritual growth, and remove the obstacles that hinder our faith.

As we reflect on this part of the parable, may we be inspired to cultivate good ground in our hearts and bear fruit for God's Kingdom. May we also be encouraged to support others in their spiritual journey, providing the guidance and encouragement needed to develop a strong foundation in their faith. And may we persevere in the work of sowing, trusting in God's faithfulness to bring about a bountiful harvest in His time.

The parable of the sower, with its description of the seeds that fell on good ground, invites us to examine our own faith journey and the ways in which we can cultivate a heart that is open, receptive, and prepared to receive God's word. It challenges us to remove the obstacles that hinder our spiritual growth and to support others in their journey. As we seek to bear fruit for the Kingdom, let us do so with faith, hope, and perseverance, trusting in God's faithfulness to bring about a bountiful harvest.

Chapter 7: The Disciples' Question

Summary: The disciples ask Jesus why He speaks to the people in parables.
Bible Verse: Matthew 13:10

As the sun began its slow descent toward the horizon, casting a warm golden glow across the fields, Jesus and His disciples found a moment of respite. The day had been filled with teaching and healing, and the crowds that had gathered to hear Jesus speak were now dispersing, each person carrying with them the seeds of His words, sown into the soil of their hearts. The disciples, ever eager to learn and understand, seized this quieter moment to ask a pressing question.

Approaching Jesus, they asked, "Why do you speak to the people in parables?" (Matthew 13:10). This question reflected their curiosity and desire for deeper understanding. Why, they wondered, did Jesus choose to communicate such profound truths through simple, often cryptic stories? What was the purpose behind this method of teaching, and how were they to understand it?

To fully explore this question, it is essential to delve into the nature and purpose of parables, the historical and cultural context in which Jesus taught, and the deeper spiritual implications of His use of parables. By examining these aspects, we can gain a richer understanding of why Jesus chose this method and what it reveals about His mission and message.

The Nature and Purpose of Parables

Parables are short, allegorical stories that convey moral or spiritual lessons. They use everyday experiences and familiar imagery to illustrate deeper truths, making abstract concepts more accessible and relatable. In the hands of a skilled teacher like Jesus, parables serve as powerful tools for communication, capable of engaging the listener's imagination and prompting deeper reflection.

One of the primary reasons Jesus used parables was to make His teachings more memorable. The human mind is naturally drawn to stories, which are easier to remember and recall than abstract concepts. By couching His teachings in the form of parables, Jesus ensured that His listeners could carry these lessons with them, pondering their meaning long after the initial hearing.

Parables also served to provoke thought and challenge the listener. Unlike straightforward statements or commands, parables require interpretation. They invite the listener to engage with the story, to seek out its meaning, and to apply it to their own lives. This process of reflection and discovery can lead to a deeper, more personal understanding of the truth being conveyed.

Moreover, parables allowed Jesus to communicate complex spiritual truths in a way that was accessible to a diverse audience. His listeners came from various backgrounds and levels of understanding, from learned religious leaders to humble fishermen. By using familiar images and scenarios, Jesus bridged the gap between these different groups, making His message accessible to all.

However, parables also had a dual purpose. While they revealed truth to those who were open and receptive, they concealed it from those who were hard-hearted or resistant. This aspect of parables is highlighted in Jesus' response to the disciples' question.

Jesus' Response to the Disciples

In response to the disciples' question, Jesus explained, "The knowledge of the secrets of the kingdom of heaven has been given to you, but not to them. Whoever has will be given more, and they will have an abundance. Whoever does not have, even what they have will be taken from them. This is why I speak to them in parables: 'Though seeing, they do not see; though hearing, they do not hear or understand'" (Matthew 13:11-13).

Jesus' explanation reveals a profound truth about the nature of His ministry and the reception of His message. The parables served to distinguish between those who were genuinely seeking the truth and those who were not. To the receptive and open-hearted, the parables were a means of revelation, drawing them closer to the mysteries of the Kingdom of Heaven. To the indifferent or hostile, the same parables remained opaque, their deeper meaning concealed.

This dual purpose of parables is rooted in the spiritual condition of the listener. Those who approached Jesus with humility and a genuine desire to learn were able to grasp the deeper truths of His teachings. Their openness allowed the Holy Spirit to illuminate their understanding, leading to greater insight and spiritual growth. Conversely, those who were proud, self-righteous, or dismissive of Jesus' message found the parables perplexing and obscure.

This dynamic reflects a broader spiritual principle: the importance of the condition of one's heart in receiving and understanding God's word. Jesus often emphasized the need for a receptive and humble heart, as seen in His teaching about the parable of the sower. The different types of soil in that parable represent the varying degrees of receptivity to God's word. Only the good soil, characterized by openness and readiness to receive, produced a fruitful harvest.

The Historical and Cultural Context

To fully appreciate the significance of Jesus' use of parables, it is helpful to consider the historical and cultural context of His ministry. Jesus taught in a time and place where storytelling was a central part of communication and education. Oral tradition was the primary means of preserving and transmitting knowledge, and stories were used to teach moral lessons, convey cultural values, and explain religious truths.

In this context, parables were a familiar and effective teaching tool. Jesus' audience would have been accustomed to hearing and interpreting stories, making them a natural vehicle for His message. The imagery and scenarios used in the parables were drawn from everyday life—agriculture, family relationships, commerce—making them relatable and accessible to His listeners.

Additionally, the use of parables allowed Jesus to navigate the complex social and political landscape of His time. His teachings often challenged the established religious and social order, confronting the hypocrisy and legalism of the religious leaders and calling for a radical reorientation of values. By using parables, Jesus could communicate these challenging truths in a way that was indirect and less confrontational, allowing His listeners to reflect on the message without immediately triggering defensive reactions.

Parables also provided a means of protection for Jesus and His followers. In a volatile political environment, where open criticism of the authorities could lead to severe repercussions, the use of parables allowed Jesus to speak truth to power in a veiled and nuanced manner. Those with ears to hear would understand the deeper implications of His teachings, while those who were hostile or indifferent might miss the subversive message.

The Spiritual Implications

The use of parables by Jesus carries significant spiritual implications for both His original audience and for us today. At its core, the parabolic method reflects the nature of God's revelation and the dynamic relationship between God and humanity.

One of the key spiritual implications of Jesus' use of parables is the concept of revelation and concealment. God's truth is not always self-evident or easily grasped; it requires a seeking heart and a willingness to delve deeper. Parables invite us into a process of discovery, encouraging us to seek and find the hidden treasures of God's wisdom. This process mirrors the journey of faith, where understanding and growth come through a continual pursuit of God's presence and truth.

The dual nature of parables—revealing to some and concealing from others—also underscores the importance of our response to God's word. The condition of our hearts determines our ability to receive and understand the message of the Kingdom. This principle is echoed throughout scripture, where humility, openness, and a genuine desire for truth are prerequisites for spiritual insight and growth.

Furthermore, the use of parables highlights the transformative power of God's word. When received with an open heart, the teachings of Jesus have the potential to change our lives, reorienting our values, priorities, and actions. The parables are not just stories to be understood intellectually; they are calls to transformation, inviting us to align our lives with the principles of the Kingdom of Heaven.

The Parables and Their Themes

To fully grasp the significance of Jesus' use of parables, it is helpful to explore some of the central themes that run through His parabolic teachings. These themes reveal the core message of Jesus and provide insight into the nature of the Kingdom of Heaven.

1. The Kingdom of Heaven: Many of Jesus' parables begin with the phrase, "The kingdom of heaven is like..." These parables offer glimpses into the nature of God's Kingdom, revealing its values, principles, and dynamics. For example, the parable of the mustard seed (Matthew 13:31-32) illustrates the Kingdom's humble beginnings and its expansive growth. The parable of the yeast (Matthew 13:33) highlights the transformative influence of the Kingdom, working invisibly but powerfully to bring about change.

2. Grace and Forgiveness: The theme of grace and forgiveness is central to many of Jesus' parables. The parable of the prodigal son (Luke 15:11-32) vividly portrays God's extravagant grace and unconditional love for sinners. The parable of the unforgiving servant (Matthew 18:21-35) emphasizes the importance of extending forgiveness to others, reflecting the forgiveness we have received from God.

3. Judgment and Accountability: Jesus' parables often include themes of judgment and accountability, reminding us of the serious consequences of our choices. The parable of the talents (Matthew 25:14-30) underscores the responsibility of stewarding God's gifts faithfully. The parable of the sheep and the goats (Matthew 25:31-46) highlights the criteria for final judgment, emphasizing the importance of compassion and service to others.

4. Discipleship and Commitment: The parables also address the cost and demands of discipleship. The parable of the sower (Matthew 13:1-23) illustrates the different responses to God's word and the necessity of a receptive heart. The parable of the rich fool (Luke 12:13-21) warns against the dangers of materialism and the need to prioritize spiritual riches.

5. Social Justice and Compassion: Jesus' parables often challenge social norms and call for a radical reorientation of values. The parable of the Good Samaritan (Luke 10:25-37) confronts prejudices and emphasizes the importance of showing mercy and compassion to all, regardless of social boundaries. The parable of the workers in the vineyard (Matthew 20:1-16) challenges notions of fairness and highlights God's generosity and grace.

Parables and the Disciples' Understanding

As the disciples listened to Jesus' response, they began to grasp the multifaceted purpose of the parables. They realized that the parables were not just teaching tools but also reflections of the deeper spiritual realities of the Kingdom. This understanding deepened their appreciation for Jesus' wisdom and the profound nature of His ministry.

The disciples' question about the parables also highlights their own journey of growth and understanding. Throughout the gospels, we see the disciples grappling with Jesus' teachings, often misunderstanding or struggling to grasp their full meaning. Yet, their willingness to ask questions and seek understanding reflects their genuine desire to learn and grow.

This dynamic of questioning and seeking understanding is a vital aspect of discipleship. Just as the disciples asked Jesus to explain the parables, we too are invited to bring our questions and seek deeper insight into God's word. This process of inquiry and exploration is a sign of a healthy and growing faith, one that is not content with surface-level understanding but seeks the deeper truths of the Kingdom.

Parables and the Modern Reader

For modern readers, the parables of Jesus continue to offer rich opportunities for reflection and growth. While the cultural and historical context may differ, the timeless truths conveyed through the parables remain relevant and transformative. To fully engage with the parables, we must approach them with the same openness and receptivity that Jesus called for in His original audience.

1. Approaching with Openness: To benefit from the parables, we must come with a heart that is open to being challenged and transformed. This means setting aside preconceived notions and allowing the parables to speak to us afresh. It involves a willingness to be surprised and to encounter the unexpected wisdom of Jesus.

2. Seeking Deeper Understanding: Engaging with the parables requires a commitment to deeper study and reflection. This involves exploring the cultural and historical context, considering different interpretations, and applying the lessons to our own lives. It may also involve seeking the guidance of trusted spiritual mentors and participating in discussions with other believers.

3. Embracing the Process: The parables invite us into a process of ongoing discovery and growth. This means being patient with ourselves as we wrestle with difficult questions and seek to apply the teachings of Jesus. It involves

recognizing that understanding and transformation are gradual and that the journey of faith is marked by continual learning and growth.

4. Applying the Lessons: The ultimate goal of engaging with the parables is to apply their lessons to our lives. This involves allowing the teachings of Jesus to shape our values, priorities, and actions. It means living out the principles of the Kingdom in our daily interactions, showing grace, compassion, and justice to others.

The Parables as a Reflection of Jesus' Mission

As we consider the disciples' question and Jesus' response, we gain insight into the broader mission of Jesus and the nature of His ministry. The parables reflect Jesus' unique approach to teaching and His deep understanding of the human heart. They reveal His commitment to reaching people where they are and inviting them into a deeper relationship with God.

The parables also highlight the inclusive and expansive nature of the Kingdom of Heaven. By using familiar images and scenarios, Jesus made the truths of the Kingdom accessible to all, regardless of their background or level of understanding. This inclusivity is a hallmark of Jesus' ministry, reflecting His desire for all people to come to know and experience the love of God.

Moreover, the parables underscore the transformative power of Jesus' message. When received with an open heart, the teachings of Jesus have the potential to bring about profound change in our lives. They challenge us to reorient our values, prioritize our relationship with God, and live out the principles of the Kingdom in our daily lives.

Conclusion

The disciples' question about the parables and Jesus' response offer a window into the heart of His ministry and the nature of His teachings. The parables are not just simple stories; they are profound vehicles of divine truth, designed to reveal and conceal, to challenge and transform. They invite us into a process of discovery and growth, calling us to seek deeper understanding and to apply their lessons to our lives.

As modern readers, we are invited to engage with the parables with openness and receptivity, seeking to uncover the timeless truths they convey. By doing so, we can experience the transformative power of Jesus' teachings and bear fruit for the Kingdom of Heaven. Let us approach the parables with humble hearts, ready to be challenged and changed, and let us strive to live out their lessons in our daily lives, reflecting the love, grace, and justice of God in all that we do.

Chapter 8: The Purpose of Parables

Summary: Jesus explains the purpose of using parables in His teachings.
Bible Verse: Matthew 13:11-13

The disciples' curiosity about Jesus' use of parables reflects a deeper quest for understanding that many of us share. Parables are a distinctive feature of Jesus' teaching, yet their purpose and function are not always immediately clear. Why did Jesus choose this method of teaching, and what did He hope to accomplish through these stories? In Matthew 13:11-13, Jesus provides insight into the purpose of parables, revealing their role in His ministry and their significance for His listeners:

"He replied, 'Because the knowledge of the secrets of the kingdom of heaven has been given to you, but not to them. Whoever has will be given more, and they will have an abundance. Whoever does not have, even what they have will be taken from them. This is why I speak to them in parables: Though seeing, they do not see; though hearing, they do not hear or understand.'"

To fully explore the purpose of parables, we will delve into several key themes: the nature of divine revelation, the role of parables in distinguishing between different types of listeners, the use of parables as a tool for both revelation and concealment, and the transformative potential of engaging with these stories. By examining these themes, we can gain a deeper understanding of why Jesus used parables and how they continue to speak to us today.

The Nature of Divine Revelation

At the heart of Jesus' explanation is the concept of divine revelation—the idea that the truths of the Kingdom of Heaven are not always immediately apparent or easily understood. Instead, they are revealed to those who are open and receptive to God's message. This principle is reflected in Jesus' words: "The knowledge of the secrets of the kingdom of heaven has been given to you, but not to them."

Divine revelation is a foundational aspect of the biblical narrative. Throughout scripture, God reveals Himself and His purposes in various ways—through creation, through the prophets, through His covenant with Israel, and ultimately through Jesus Christ. This revelation is both a gift and a responsibility, calling those who receive it to respond in faith and obedience.

The use of parables aligns with this pattern of revelation. Parables are not straightforward explanations or doctrinal statements; they are stories that invite listeners to engage with the deeper truths of God's Kingdom. By using parables, Jesus encourages His listeners to seek, to reflect, and to discover the hidden treasures of divine wisdom.

This approach reflects the relational nature of God's revelation. God does not merely dispense information; He invites us into a dynamic relationship, where understanding grows through interaction and engagement. Parables are a means of fostering this relational process, drawing us into a deeper exploration of God's character and His Kingdom.

Distinguishing Between Listeners

Another key aspect of Jesus' explanation is the distinction between different types of listeners. The parables serve as a means of distinguishing between those who are open and receptive to God's word and those who are not. Jesus' statement—"Whoever has will be given more, and they will have an abundance. Whoever does not have, even what they have will be taken from them"—highlights this dynamic.

This principle of distinguishing between listeners is evident in the varied responses to Jesus' teachings throughout the Gospels. Some individuals responded with faith and obedience, while others reacted with skepticism, hostility, or indifference. The parables, with their layers of meaning, reflect and reinforce these differing responses.

To those who are open and seeking, the parables are a source of deeper understanding. The stories resonate with their experiences, prompting reflection and insight. The imagery and scenarios used in the parables draw them into a process of discovery, where the truths of the Kingdom become clearer and more compelling.

Conversely, to those who are resistant or indifferent, the parables remain enigmatic. Their lack of receptivity prevents them from grasping the deeper meanings embedded in the stories. This dynamic reflects a broader spiritual principle: the condition of our hearts determines our ability to receive and understand God's word.

This distinction between listeners is not a matter of intellectual ability but of spiritual openness. The parables reveal the importance of approaching God's word with humility, readiness, and a genuine desire for truth. Those who possess these qualities are able to uncover the treasures hidden within the parables, while those who lack them remain in spiritual darkness.

Revelation and Concealment

Jesus' explanation also highlights the dual purpose of parables as tools for both revelation and concealment. He states, "This is why I speak to them in parables: Though seeing, they do not see; though hearing, they do not hear or understand." This paradoxical dynamic is a central feature of the parables, reflecting the complex nature of divine revelation.

On one hand, parables reveal profound truths about the Kingdom of Heaven. They use familiar imagery and scenarios to illustrate spiritual principles, making abstract concepts more accessible and relatable. For those who are open and receptive, the parables are a source of illumination, shedding light on the mysteries of God's Kingdom.

On the other hand, parables also serve to conceal these truths from those who are not receptive. The stories are not immediately transparent; they require reflection and engagement to uncover their deeper meanings. This aspect of concealment serves as a form of judgment on those who are spiritually resistant or indifferent, highlighting the consequences of their lack of openness.

This dual purpose of revelation and concealment reflects a broader biblical theme: the mystery of God's Kingdom. The Kingdom of Heaven is both revealed and hidden, accessible and elusive. It is revealed to those who seek it with humility and faith, but hidden from those who are self-sufficient or dismissive.

This dynamic is evident in Jesus' interactions with various individuals and groups throughout the Gospels. To those who approached Him with genuine faith and a desire for truth, Jesus offered deeper insight and understanding. To those who were skeptical or hostile, He often responded with parables that left them puzzled and challenged.

The Transformative Potential of Parables

One of the most significant aspects of parables is their transformative potential. Parables are not just stories to be understood intellectually; they are calls to transformation, inviting us to align our lives with the principles of the Kingdom of Heaven. This transformative potential is rooted in the power of God's word to change hearts and minds.

Parables engage the listener's imagination and prompt reflection. By using vivid imagery and relatable scenarios, Jesus draws His listeners into a process of discovery. The stories invite us to see ourselves within them, to identify with the characters and their experiences. This process of identification can lead to self-examination and a deeper understanding of our own spiritual condition.

Moreover, parables often challenge our assumptions and values. They confront us with the radical nature of God's Kingdom, calling us to reorient our priorities and actions. For example, the parable of the Good Samaritan (Luke 10:25-37) challenges our prejudices and calls us to show mercy and compassion to all, regardless of social boundaries. The parable of the prodigal son (Luke 15:11-32) confronts our notions of justice and grace, revealing the extravagant love of God for sinners.

The transformative potential of parables is also evident in their ability to provoke action. Many of Jesus' parables conclude with a call to response, inviting us to apply the lessons to our lives. The parable of the talents (Matthew 25:14-30) calls us to be faithful stewards of God's gifts, while the parable of the sheep and the goats (Matthew 25:31-46) emphasizes the importance of compassionate service to others.

By engaging with parables, we are invited into a dynamic process of growth and transformation. The stories challenge us to examine our hearts, to seek deeper understanding, and to live out the principles of the Kingdom in our daily lives. This transformative potential is a key aspect of the purpose of parables, reflecting Jesus' desire for His followers to experience the fullness of God's Kingdom.

The Parables in the Context of Jesus' Ministry

To fully appreciate the purpose of parables, it is important to consider them in the context of Jesus' overall ministry. Jesus' use of parables was not an isolated teaching technique but an integral part of His mission to proclaim the Kingdom of Heaven.

Throughout His ministry, Jesus used parables to communicate the radical nature of God's Kingdom. The parables challenged the established religious and social order, calling for a reorientation of values and priorities. They confronted the hypocrisy and legalism of the religious leaders, offering a vision of the Kingdom that was inclusive, compassionate, and transformative.

The parables also served as a means of protecting Jesus and His followers in a volatile political environment. By using indirect and symbolic language, Jesus could communicate challenging truths without immediately provoking the authorities. This approach allowed Him to speak truth to power in a nuanced and strategic manner, revealing the subversive nature of God's Kingdom while avoiding direct confrontation.

Moreover, the parables reflect Jesus' deep understanding of the human heart. He knew that true understanding and transformation could not be achieved through mere information or coercion. Instead, He invited His listeners into a process of discovery and reflection, allowing them to encounter the truths of the Kingdom in a personal and transformative way.

The use of parables also highlights the relational nature of Jesus' ministry. Jesus did not merely impart knowledge; He invited His followers into a dynamic relationship with Him and with God. The parables fostered this relational process, encouraging His listeners to seek, to ask, and to engage with the deeper truths of the Kingdom.

Parables and the Modern Reader

For modern readers, the parables of Jesus continue to offer rich opportunities for reflection and growth. While the cultural and historical context may differ, the timeless truths conveyed through the parables remain relevant and transformative. To fully engage with the parables, we must approach them with the same openness and receptivity that

Jesus called for in His original audience.

1. Approaching with Openness: To benefit from the parables, we must come with a heart that is open to being challenged and transformed. This means setting aside preconceived notions and allowing the parables to speak to us afresh. It involves a willingness to be surprised and to encounter the unexpected wisdom of Jesus.

2. Seeking Deeper Understanding: Engaging with the parables requires a commitment to deeper study and reflection. This involves exploring the cultural and historical context, considering different interpretations, and applying the lessons to our own lives. It may also involve seeking the guidance of trusted spiritual mentors and participating in discussions with other believers.

3. Embracing the Process: The parables invite us into a process of ongoing discovery and growth. This means being patient with ourselves as we wrestle with difficult questions and seek to apply the teachings of Jesus. It involves recognizing that understanding and transformation are gradual and that the journey of faith is marked by continual learning and growth.

4. Applying the Lessons: The ultimate goal of engaging with the parables is to apply their lessons to our lives. This involves allowing the teachings of Jesus to shape our values, priorities, and actions. It means living out the principles of the Kingdom in our daily interactions, showing grace, compassion, and justice to others.

Conclusion

The purpose of parables, as explained by Jesus in Matthew 13:11-13, reveals the multifaceted nature of His teaching method and the profound spiritual dynamics at play. Parables serve as tools for both revelation and concealment, distinguishing between different types of listeners and inviting us into a process of discovery and transformation. They reflect the relational nature of God's revelation and the radical nature of His Kingdom.

For modern readers, the parables of Jesus continue to offer rich opportunities for reflection and growth. By approaching the parables with openness and receptivity, seeking deeper understanding, embracing the process of discovery, and applying their lessons to our lives, we can experience the transformative power of Jesus' teachings and bear fruit for the Kingdom of Heaven.

As we engage with the parables, let us do so with humble hearts, ready to be challenged and changed. Let us seek to uncover the timeless truths they convey and to live out their lessons in our daily lives. In doing so, we can experience the fullness of God's Kingdom and reflect His love, grace, and justice in all that we do.

Chapter 9: The Prophecy Fulfilled

Summary: Jesus cites Isaiah's prophecy about people who hear but do not understand.

Bible Verse: Matthew 13:14-15

As the day drew to a close and the golden hues of sunset bathed the landscape, Jesus continued to teach His disciples, revealing deeper truths about His mission and the Kingdom of Heaven. One of the most significant moments in His explanation of why He used parables was His reference to the prophecy of Isaiah. In Matthew 13:14-15, Jesus cites this prophecy to explain the spiritual condition of the people and to underscore the fulfillment of God's word through His ministry:

"In them is fulfilled the prophecy of Isaiah: 'You will be ever hearing but never understanding; you will be ever seeing but never perceiving. For this people's heart has become calloused; they hardly hear with their ears, and they have closed their eyes. Otherwise they might see with their eyes, hear with their ears, understand with their hearts and turn, and I would heal them.'"

To fully appreciate the significance of this reference, it is essential to explore the context and meaning of Isaiah's prophecy, the reasons Jesus invoked it, and the broader implications for His ministry and for us today. This chapter will delve into these themes, offering a comprehensive understanding of the prophecy fulfilled in Jesus' use of parables.

The Context of Isaiah's Prophecy

The prophecy that Jesus cites comes from Isaiah 6:9-10, a passage that is pivotal in the narrative of the prophet Isaiah's calling and commission. Isaiah, a prophet in the 8th century BCE, was called by God during a time of national crisis and spiritual decline in Israel. The northern kingdom of Israel faced the threat of Assyrian invasion, and the southern kingdom of Judah was mired in idolatry and injustice.

Isaiah's vision of God's holiness and majesty, described in Isaiah 6, is a dramatic and awe-inspiring scene. In this vision, Isaiah sees the Lord seated on a high and exalted throne, with seraphim attending Him and proclaiming,

"Holy, holy, holy is the Lord Almighty; the whole earth is full of his glory" (Isaiah 6:3). Overwhelmed by the sight of God's glory and his own unworthiness, Isaiah laments, "Woe to me!... I am ruined! For I am a man of unclean lips, and I live among a people of unclean lips, and my eyes have seen the King, the Lord Almighty" (Isaiah 6:5).

In response to Isaiah's confession, one of the seraphim touches his lips with a live coal from the altar, symbolizing his cleansing and forgiveness. Then, God issues a call, asking, "Whom shall I send? And who will go for us?" Isaiah responds with a willing heart, saying, "Here am I. Send me!" (Isaiah 6:8).

It is in this context that God commissions Isaiah and delivers the prophecy that Jesus later quotes. God tells Isaiah, "Go and tell this people: 'Be ever hearing, but never understanding; be ever seeing, but never perceiving.' Make the heart of this people calloused; make their ears dull and close their eyes. Otherwise they might see with their eyes, hear with their ears, understand with their hearts, and turn and be healed" (Isaiah 6:9-10).

This prophecy reflects the tragic spiritual condition of the people of Israel. Despite God's repeated attempts to reach them through the prophets, their hearts had become hardened, and they were unwilling to listen and repent. God's message, delivered through Isaiah, would serve to further expose and solidify their obstinance, leading to judgment and exile.

Jesus' Invocation of Isaiah's Prophecy

When Jesus cited Isaiah's prophecy in Matthew 13:14-15, He was drawing a parallel between the spiritual condition of the people in Isaiah's time and those in His own day. Just as the people of Israel in Isaiah's time were spiritually blind and deaf, so too were many of the people who heard Jesus' teachings. Despite witnessing His miracles and hearing His words, their hearts remained hardened, and they failed to understand and respond.

Jesus' use of parables was directly linked to this spiritual condition. The parables, with their layers of meaning, served both to reveal and to conceal truth. To those who were open and receptive, the parables offered insight into the mysteries of the Kingdom of Heaven. But to those who were hard-hearted and resistant, the parables remained enigmatic and obscure.

By invoking Isaiah's prophecy, Jesus was not only explaining the purpose of His parables but also fulfilling the prophetic word. His ministry was a continuation of God's ongoing revelation and judgment, highlighting the persistent issue of human resistance to divine truth.

The Spiritual Condition of the People

The prophecy of Isaiah, as cited by Jesus, provides a sobering assessment of the spiritual condition of the people: "For this people's heart has become calloused; they hardly hear with their ears, and they have closed their eyes." This description of a calloused heart, dull ears, and closed eyes captures the essence of spiritual insensitivity and resistance.

A calloused heart refers to a heart that has become hardened and unresponsive. Just as physical calluses form through repeated friction and pressure, spiritual calluses develop through persistent resistance to God's word and Spirit. This hardening of the heart leads to a diminished ability to perceive and respond to spiritual truths.

The imagery of dull ears and closed eyes further illustrates this condition. Dull ears suggest a lack of attentiveness and sensitivity to God's voice, while closed eyes indicate a refusal to see and acknowledge the truth. Together, these images portray a state of spiritual insensitivity that prevents true understanding and transformation.

Jesus' invocation of this prophecy underscores the seriousness of this spiritual condition. It is not merely a matter of intellectual misunderstanding but a deep-seated resistance that affects the core of one's being. This resistance prevents individuals from experiencing the healing and transformation that come from truly understanding and responding to God's word.

The Consequences of Spiritual Insensitivity

The prophecy from Isaiah, as cited by Jesus, also highlights the consequences of spiritual insensitivity: "Otherwise they might see with their eyes, hear with their ears, understand with their hearts and turn, and I would heal them." This statement reveals the tragic irony of the people's condition. The very healing and transformation they need are available to them, but their resistance prevents them from receiving it.

The consequences of spiritual insensitivity are multifaceted. On a personal level, it results in a lack of spiritual growth and transformation. Without true understanding and responsiveness to God's word, individuals remain trapped in patterns of sin and brokenness. They miss out on the abundant life that Jesus offers and the healing and restoration that come from a deep relationship with God.

On a communal level, spiritual insensitivity affects the broader community and society. The lack of responsiveness to God's word leads to a breakdown in justice, compassion, and righteousness. In Isaiah's time, this manifested in social injustices, idolatry, and moral decay. In Jesus' time, it was evident in the hypocrisy and legalism of the religious leaders and the oppression and marginalization of the vulnerable.

The consequences of spiritual insensitivity also extend to the eternal realm. Jesus' teachings often emphasized the reality of judgment and the need for repentance. The failure to respond to God's word results in spiritual separation from God and the loss of eternal life. This sobering reality underscores the urgency of cultivating a receptive and responsive heart.

The Role of Parables in Addressing Spiritual Insensitivity

Given the seriousness of spiritual insensitivity, Jesus' use of parables takes on even greater significance. The parables serve as a divine strategy to address this condition, offering both a challenge and an invitation.

On one hand, the parables challenge the listeners to reflect on their own spiritual condition. The stories often include characters and scenarios that mirror the listeners' own lives and attitudes. By inviting the listeners to see themselves within the story, the parables prompt self-examination and a recognition of their need for transformation.

For example, the parable of the sower (Matthew 13:1-23) challenges listeners to consider the condition of their own hearts in receiving God's word. The different types of soil represent various responses to the message of the

Kingdom, inviting listeners to reflect on whether their hearts are like the hard path, the rocky ground, the thorny soil, or the good soil.

Similarly, the parable of the prodigal son (Luke 15:11-32) invites listeners to see themselves in the characters of the younger son, who rebels and repents, and the older son, who struggles with self-righteousness and resentment. The story highlights the themes of repentance, forgiveness, and the extravagant love of the Father, calling listeners to examine their own attitudes and relationships.

On the other hand, the parables offer an invitation to deeper understanding and transformation. For those who are open and receptive, the stories provide a pathway to discover the truths of the Kingdom of Heaven. The imagery and scenarios used in the parables engage the imagination and prompt reflection, allowing the listeners to uncover the deeper meanings and apply them to their own lives.

The parables also create a space for ongoing discovery and growth. Unlike straightforward statements or commands, the stories invite repeated engagement and reflection. As listeners return to the parables, they can uncover new insights and apply the lessons in fresh ways, leading to continuous spiritual growth and transformation.

The Broader Implications for Jesus' Ministry

Jesus' citation of Isaiah's prophecy and His use of parables also have broader implications for understanding His ministry and mission. The fulfillment of Isaiah's prophecy through Jesus' teachings highlights several key themes that are central to His work.

1. Continuity with the Prophetic Tradition: By citing Isaiah's prophecy, Jesus places His ministry within the broader context of the prophetic tradition. Just as the prophets called the people to repentance and revealed God's judgment and mercy, Jesus continues this mission, calling His listeners to respond to the message of the Kingdom of Heaven.

2. Judgment and Mercy: The use of parables to reveal and conceal truth reflects the dual themes of judgment and mercy. Those who are receptive to the message of the Kingdom experience the mercy and grace of God, while those who are resistant face the consequences of their spiritual insensitivity. This

dynamic underscores the seriousness of the call to repentance and the urgency of responding to God's word.

3. Invitation to Relationship: The parables also highlight Jesus' desire for a relational and transformative engagement with His listeners. By inviting them into a process of discovery and reflection, Jesus calls them into a deeper relationship with Him and with God. This relational approach contrasts with mere intellectual assent or ritual compliance, emphasizing the heart's response to God's love and truth.

4. The Inclusivity of the Kingdom: The parables often highlight the inclusive nature of the Kingdom of Heaven, challenging social and religious boundaries. Stories like the parable of the Good Samaritan (Luke 10:25-37) and the parable of the workers in the vineyard (Matthew 20:1-16) reveal the expansive and generous nature of God's grace, inviting all to participate in the Kingdom.

Engaging with the Parables Today

For modern readers, the parables of Jesus continue to offer rich opportunities for reflection and transformation. By approaching the parables with openness and receptivity, we can uncover the timeless truths they convey and apply their lessons to our lives.

1. Approaching with Humility: To engage with the parables, we must come with a humble heart, ready to be challenged and transformed. This means setting aside preconceived notions and allowing the stories to speak to us afresh. It involves a willingness to be surprised and to encounter the unexpected wisdom of Jesus.

2. Seeking Deeper Understanding: Engaging with the parables requires a commitment to deeper study and reflection. This involves exploring the cultural and historical context, considering different interpretations, and applying the lessons to our own lives. It may also involve seeking the guidance of trusted spiritual mentors and participating in discussions with other believers.

3. Embracing the Process of Discovery: The parables invite us into a process of ongoing discovery and growth. This means being patient with ourselves as we wrestle with difficult questions and seek to apply the teachings of Jesus. It

involves recognizing that understanding and transformation are gradual and that the journey of faith is marked by continual learning and growth.

4. Applying the Lessons: The ultimate goal of engaging with the parables is to apply their lessons to our lives. This involves allowing the teachings of Jesus to shape our values, priorities, and actions. It means living out the principles of the Kingdom in our daily interactions, showing grace, compassion, and justice to others.

5. Reflecting on Our Own Spiritual Condition: The parables also invite us to reflect on our own spiritual condition and to examine the areas where we may be resistant or insensitive to God's word. By identifying and addressing these areas, we can cultivate a more receptive and responsive heart, open to the transformative power of God's word.

Conclusion

The prophecy of Isaiah, as cited by Jesus in Matthew 13:14-15, provides a profound and sobering assessment of the spiritual condition of the people and the purpose of Jesus' use of parables. The parables serve both to reveal and to conceal truth, distinguishing between different types of listeners and inviting us into a process of discovery and transformation.

By invoking Isaiah's prophecy, Jesus highlights the continuity of His ministry with the prophetic tradition and underscores the seriousness of the call to repentance and responsiveness to God's word. The parables challenge us to reflect on our own spiritual condition, to seek deeper understanding, and to live out the principles of the Kingdom in our daily lives.

For modern readers, the parables of Jesus continue to offer rich opportunities for reflection and growth. By approaching the parables with humility and openness, seeking deeper understanding, embracing the process of discovery, and applying their lessons to our lives, we can experience the transformative power of Jesus' teachings and bear fruit for the Kingdom of Heaven.

As we engage with the parables, let us do so with a humble heart, ready to be challenged and changed. Let us seek to uncover the timeless truths they convey and to live out their lessons in our daily lives. In doing so, we can experience the fullness of God's Kingdom and reflect His love, grace, and justice in all that we do.

Chapter 10: Blessed Are Your Eyes

Summary: Jesus tells His disciples that they are blessed to see and hear what many prophets and righteous people longed to see and hear.

Bible Verse: Matthew 13:16-17

As the sun set on the horizon, casting long shadows and a golden glow over the landscape, Jesus gathered His disciples around Him. The day had been filled with teaching, parables, and interactions with the crowds. Now, in this quieter moment, He turned to His closest followers and spoke words of profound significance: "But blessed are your eyes because they see, and your ears because they hear. For truly I tell you, many prophets and righteous people longed to see what you see but did not see it, and to hear what you hear but did not hear it" (Matthew 13:16-17).

These words were not only a statement of fact but a deep affirmation of the unique and privileged position the disciples held. To understand the full depth of Jesus' statement, we need to explore several key themes: the historical and prophetic context, the nature of the blessings bestowed upon the disciples, the fulfillment of long-awaited promises, and the implications for us today as followers of Jesus.

The Historical and Prophetic Context

The statement that Jesus made to His disciples is rooted in a rich historical and prophetic context. Throughout the history of Israel, prophets and righteous people had received glimpses of God's redemptive plan and had longed for its fulfillment. They spoke of a coming Messiah, a time of restoration, and the establishment of God's Kingdom. These prophetic visions were often accompanied by a sense of anticipation and yearning.

1. The Prophets' Vision: Prophets like Isaiah, Jeremiah, Ezekiel, and Daniel received revelations about the coming Messiah and the future Kingdom of God. Isaiah spoke of a suffering servant who would bear the sins of many (Isaiah 53), a child who would be called Wonderful Counselor, Mighty God, Everlasting Father, Prince of Peace (Isaiah 9:6). Jeremiah prophesied about a new covenant written on the hearts of God's people (Jeremiah 31:31-34).

Ezekiel had visions of a restored Israel and a new heart and spirit (Ezekiel 36:26-28). Daniel foresaw the establishment of an everlasting Kingdom (Daniel 2:44).

2. The Longing of the Righteous: Beyond the prophets, many righteous individuals in Israel's history longed to see the fulfillment of God's promises. Figures like Abraham, Moses, David, and others had personal encounters with God and were given promises about the future. Abraham was promised that through his offspring all nations would be blessed (Genesis 12:3). Moses looked forward to a prophet like himself who would lead God's people (Deuteronomy 18:15). David was given a covenant that his throne would be established forever (2 Samuel 7:16).

3. The Period of Waiting: Despite these promises and visions, there was a long period of waiting and often suffering. Israel experienced exile, oppression, and periods of silence from God. The intertestamental period, between the Old and New Testaments, was marked by a sense of anticipation and longing for the fulfillment of the Messianic prophecies.

Against this backdrop, Jesus' words to His disciples take on profound significance. The disciples were witnessing the fulfillment of centuries of prophetic expectation. They were seeing and hearing what generations before them had longed for but did not experience in their lifetimes.

The Nature of the Blessings Bestowed Upon the Disciples

Jesus' statement, "Blessed are your eyes because they see, and your ears because they hear," highlights the unique blessings bestowed upon the disciples. To fully appreciate this, we need to explore what it meant for the disciples to see and hear the things they did and how these experiences shaped their understanding and faith.

1. Seeing the Messiah: The disciples had the incredible privilege of seeing Jesus, the Messiah, in the flesh. They witnessed His miracles, His compassion, His authority over nature, sickness, and even death. They saw Him transfigured on the mountain, revealing His divine glory (Matthew 17:1-8). They experienced His resurrection, the ultimate confirmation of His identity and mission (John 20:19-29).

2. Hearing the Words of Life: The disciples heard Jesus' teachings firsthand. They listened to the Sermon on the Mount, where Jesus expounded on the values of the Kingdom of Heaven (Matthew 5-7). They heard His parables, which revealed deep spiritual truths. They received private explanations and insights that were not given to the general public (Matthew 13:10-17).

3. Experiencing the Kingdom: The disciples were not only observers but participants in the unfolding of God's Kingdom. Jesus sent them out to proclaim the good news, heal the sick, and cast out demons (Matthew 10:1-8). They were witnesses to the breaking in of God's reign, as lives were transformed and signs of the Kingdom were manifested.

4. Receiving the Holy Spirit: After Jesus' resurrection and ascension, the disciples received the Holy Spirit at Pentecost (Acts 2:1-4). This outpouring of the Spirit empowered them to continue Jesus' mission, to preach the gospel with boldness, and to perform signs and wonders in His name. The Holy Spirit also provided them with guidance, comfort, and a deeper understanding of Jesus' teachings (John 14:26).

The blessings of seeing and hearing that Jesus referred to were not just about physical sight and hearing but about spiritual insight and understanding. The disciples were given the privilege of experiencing God's redemptive plan in a unique and transformative way.

The Fulfillment of Long-Awaited Promises

Jesus' ministry represented the fulfillment of the long-awaited promises of God. This fulfillment was not just about specific prophecies but about the overarching narrative of God's plan for redemption and restoration.

1. The Coming of the Messiah: Jesus' arrival fulfilled the Messianic prophecies that had been spoken for centuries. He was the promised one who would bring salvation and establish God's Kingdom. His life, death, and resurrection were the culmination of God's redemptive plan.

2. The New Covenant: Jesus inaugurated the new covenant that Jeremiah had prophesied. Through His sacrificial death, He established a new relationship between God and humanity, characterized by forgiveness of sins and the indwelling of the Holy Spirit. This new covenant was marked by a

transformation of the heart and a direct, personal relationship with God (Hebrews 8:8-12).

3. The Kingdom of God: Jesus' ministry demonstrated the breaking in of God's Kingdom. His miracles, teachings, and authority over evil spirits were signs of the Kingdom's presence. He called people to repentance and faith, inviting them to enter into the reality of God's reign (Mark 1:15).

4. The Universal Blessing: The promise to Abraham that through his offspring all nations would be blessed found its fulfillment in Jesus. The gospel message was not limited to Israel but was extended to all peoples. The disciples were commissioned to go and make disciples of all nations (Matthew 28:19), fulfilling the promise of universal blessing.

The fulfillment of these promises was a cause for great joy and gratitude. The disciples were living in a time of unprecedented spiritual significance, witnessing the realization of God's redemptive purposes.

The Implications for Modern Believers

While the disciples were uniquely blessed to see and hear what they did, Jesus' words have implications for modern believers as well. As followers of Jesus today, we too are recipients of the blessings of His redemptive work and the ongoing presence of the Holy Spirit.

1. Access to Revelation: Through the scriptures, we have access to the revelation of God's redemptive plan. The New Testament provides a detailed account of Jesus' life, teachings, death, and resurrection. We can study the words of Jesus and the writings of the apostles, gaining insight into the mysteries of the Kingdom of Heaven.

2. The Presence of the Holy Spirit: Like the disciples, we have the Holy Spirit dwelling within us. The Spirit guides us into all truth, helps us understand the scriptures, and empowers us to live out the teachings of Jesus. The presence of the Holy Spirit is a continuous source of comfort, guidance, and strength (John 14:16-17).

3. Participation in the Kingdom: As believers, we are invited to participate in the mission of the Kingdom. We are called to share the good news of Jesus, to serve others, and to live out the values of the Kingdom in our daily lives. This

participation is both a privilege and a responsibility, as we seek to reflect God's love and justice in the world.

4. Hope of Future Fulfillment: While we experience the blessings of the Kingdom now, we also look forward to its future fulfillment. The promises of God will be fully realized when Jesus returns, bringing about the complete restoration of all things. This hope sustains us and motivates us to live faithfully in the present.

Living with Gratitude and Responsibility

Understanding the unique blessings we have as followers of Jesus should lead us to live with both gratitude and a sense of responsibility. The disciples' experience of seeing and hearing the fulfillment of God's promises is a reminder of the incredible privilege we have in being part of God's redemptive story.

1. Gratitude: We are called to live with deep gratitude for the grace and mercy we have received. The knowledge of God's redemptive plan and the presence of the Holy Spirit are gifts that should inspire thankfulness and worship. Reflecting on the faithfulness of God throughout history can deepen our appreciation for His work in our lives.

2. Responsibility: Along with the blessings we receive comes the responsibility to share those blessings with others. Just as the disciples were commissioned to proclaim the good news, we too are called to be witnesses of Jesus' love and grace. This involves both words and actions, as we seek to reflect the character of Christ in all we do.

3. Continual Growth: The disciples' journey with Jesus was marked by continual growth and learning. As modern believers, we are also on a journey of spiritual growth. This means engaging with the scriptures, seeking the guidance of the Holy Spirit, and being open to transformation. Spiritual growth is a lifelong process that requires intentionality and commitment.

4. Community and Fellowship: The disciples experienced the blessings of seeing and hearing in the context of community. As believers, we are part of the body of Christ, and our journey of faith is meant to be shared with others. Fellowship with other believers provides support, encouragement, and accountability. It is within the community of faith that we can grow, serve, and fulfill our calling.

Reflecting on the Prophetic Witness

The words of Jesus in Matthew 13:16-17 also invite us to reflect on the prophetic witness of those who came before us. The prophets and righteous individuals in Israel's history were faithful to their calling, often in the face of great adversity. Their witness provides valuable lessons for us as we seek to live faithfully in our own time.

1. Faithfulness in Waiting: The prophets and righteous people demonstrated faithfulness in waiting for the fulfillment of God's promises. They remained steadfast in their trust in God, even when the fulfillment seemed distant or uncertain. This example encourages us to remain faithful in our own times of waiting, trusting that God's timing is perfect.

2. Courage in Proclamation: Many of the prophets faced opposition and persecution for their message. Their courage in proclaiming God's word, even in difficult circumstances, is a powerful example for us. As we seek to share the gospel and live out our faith, we can draw strength from their example of boldness and perseverance.

3. Hope in God's Promises: The prophets and righteous individuals held on to the hope of God's promises, even when they did not see their fulfillment in their lifetime. This hope sustained them and gave them a future-oriented perspective. As believers, we too hold on to the hope of God's promises, looking forward to the ultimate fulfillment of His redemptive plan.

The Privilege of Revelation

Jesus' words to His disciples remind us of the privilege of revelation. The knowledge of God's redemptive plan, the presence of the Holy Spirit, and the opportunity to participate in the Kingdom are incredible gifts. These privileges call us to a life of gratitude, responsibility, and faithful witness.

As we reflect on the blessings of seeing and hearing, let us be mindful of the responsibility that comes with these gifts. May we live with a sense of purpose and intentionality, seeking to glorify God in all we do. Let us also be encouraged by the examples of the prophets and righteous individuals who came before us, drawing strength from their faithfulness and hope.

In conclusion, Jesus' statement to His disciples in Matthew 13:16-17 highlights the unique and privileged position they held in witnessing the fulfillment of God's promises. This privilege extends to us as modern believers, as we have access to the revelation of God's redemptive plan and the ongoing presence of the Holy Spirit. Let us live with gratitude, responsibility, and a commitment to sharing the blessings we have received with others. In doing so, we can experience the fullness of God's Kingdom and reflect His love, grace, and justice in the world.

Chapter 11: The Explanation of the Wayside

Summary: Jesus explains that the seeds by the wayside represent those who hear the word but do not understand it, and the evil one comes and snatches away what was sown.

Bible Verse: Matthew 13:18-19

As the sun dipped below the horizon, painting the sky with hues of orange and pink, Jesus gathered His disciples close, ready to provide deeper insight into His teachings. The parable of the sower had left many in the crowd pondering its meaning, but now, in the quiet of the evening, Jesus offered His disciples an explanation that would clarify the spiritual truths He had been conveying.

"Listen then to what the parable of the sower means: When anyone hears the message about the kingdom and does not understand it, the evil one comes and snatches away what was sown in their heart. This is the seed sown along the path" (Matthew 13:18-19).

In this chapter, we will explore Jesus' explanation of the wayside in the parable of the sower. We will delve into the nature of spiritual understanding, the challenges that prevent comprehension, and the malevolent forces that seek to undermine the reception of God's word. Additionally, we will consider practical applications for cultivating a receptive heart and the broader implications for discipleship and spiritual growth.

The Nature of Spiritual Understanding

At the core of Jesus' explanation is the concept of understanding. The seeds that fall by the wayside represent those who hear the message of the Kingdom but do not understand it. This lack of understanding is not merely intellectual but spiritual, involving the heart and mind in a comprehensive grasp of God's truth.

1. Intellectual vs. Spiritual Understanding: Intellectual understanding involves the cognitive process of grasping facts and concepts. While important, it is insufficient for spiritual transformation. Spiritual understanding goes deeper, engaging the heart and will, leading to a transformative relationship

with God. Jesus often emphasized the need for this deeper understanding, calling His followers to perceive the spiritual realities behind His teachings.

2. The Role of the Heart: In biblical terms, the heart is the center of one's being, encompassing emotions, desires, and will. Spiritual understanding requires a receptive heart, one that is open to God's word and willing to be transformed by it. This receptivity involves humility, a willingness to be taught, and a desire to align one's life with God's will.

3. The Process of Revelation: Understanding the message of the Kingdom is a process facilitated by the Holy Spirit. Jesus promised that the Spirit would guide His followers into all truth (John 16:13). This guidance involves illuminating the scriptures, convicting of sin, and revealing the beauty and worth of Christ. It is through the Spirit's work that true spiritual understanding is achieved.

Challenges to Comprehension

Several challenges can prevent individuals from understanding the message of the Kingdom. These obstacles are multifaceted, involving personal, cultural, and spiritual dimensions.

1. Personal Obstacles: Personal obstacles to understanding include pride, apathy, and preconceived notions. Pride prevents individuals from acknowledging their need for God's wisdom, while apathy leads to a lack of interest in spiritual matters. Preconceived notions can blind individuals to new truths, causing them to reject teachings that challenge their existing beliefs.

2. Cultural Influences: Cultural influences can shape one's receptivity to the gospel. In a culture that values materialism, secularism, or relativism, the message of the Kingdom can seem irrelevant or counterintuitive. These cultural narratives can create barriers to understanding, making it difficult for individuals to see the value and truth of God's word.

3. Spiritual Warfare: Jesus' explanation highlights the role of the evil one in preventing comprehension. Spiritual warfare is a reality in the Christian life, with malevolent forces actively working to hinder the reception of God's word. Satan's tactics include distraction, deception, and discouragement, all aimed at keeping individuals from understanding and embracing the gospel.

The Role of the Evil One

Jesus specifically mentions the evil one who comes and snatches away what was sown in the heart. This imagery underscores the active opposition of Satan to God's redemptive work.

1. Satan's Opposition: Satan's primary goal is to thwart God's purposes and prevent people from entering into a saving relationship with Him. This opposition is evident throughout scripture, from the temptation of Adam and Eve in the Garden of Eden to the temptations of Jesus in the wilderness. Satan's tactics are varied and insidious, targeting individuals' weaknesses and exploiting their vulnerabilities.

2. The Snatching Away of the Word: The imagery of the evil one snatching away the seed highlights the immediacy and urgency of his actions. As soon as the word is sown, Satan seeks to remove it before it can take root and grow. This can happen through distraction, where individuals become preoccupied with other concerns, or through doubt, where individuals question the truth and relevance of the gospel.

3. The Battle for the Mind: Spiritual warfare often centers on the mind, where thoughts and beliefs are formed. Satan aims to fill minds with lies and half-truths, creating confusion and doubt. The apostle Paul exhorted believers to take every thought captive to obey Christ (2 Corinthians 10:5), recognizing the importance of a mind renewed by God's truth.

Practical Applications for Cultivating a Receptive Heart

Given the challenges to understanding and the active opposition of the evil one, it is crucial to cultivate a receptive heart. Here are several practical steps to foster spiritual understanding and protect against the snatching away of God's word.

1. Prayer for Understanding: Prayer is essential in seeking spiritual understanding. We can ask God to open our hearts and minds to His truth, to remove any obstacles, and to protect us from the evil one. The psalmist's prayer, "Open my eyes that I may see wonderful things in your law" (Psalm 119:18), is a model for our own prayers for illumination.

2. Engagement with Scripture: Regular and intentional engagement with scripture is vital for spiritual growth. This involves not only reading the Bible but also meditating on its truths, studying its context, and applying its teachings to our lives. Scripture memorization can also be a powerful tool in guarding against the evil one's tactics.

3. Community and Accountability: Being part of a faith community provides support and encouragement in our spiritual journey. Fellow believers can offer insights, ask challenging questions, and hold us accountable in our walk with Christ. Small groups, Bible studies, and discipleship relationships are valuable contexts for deepening our understanding and growth.

4. Humility and Teachability: Cultivating a receptive heart requires humility and a willingness to be taught. We must recognize our need for God's wisdom and be open to learning from others, whether through sermons, books, or conversations. This attitude of humility creates fertile ground for God's word to take root and grow.

5. Discernment and Vigilance: Given the reality of spiritual warfare, we must be vigilant and discerning. This involves being aware of the ways in which Satan seeks to undermine our faith and taking proactive steps to guard against his tactics. Putting on the full armor of God (Ephesians 6:10-18) is a practical way to stand firm in the face of spiritual opposition.

The Broader Implications for Discipleship and Spiritual Growth

Jesus' explanation of the wayside has broader implications for discipleship and spiritual growth. Understanding the dynamics of spiritual receptivity and opposition can inform our approach to evangelism, teaching, and personal spiritual development.

1. Approach to Evangelism: In evangelism, recognizing the challenges to comprehension and the role of the evil one can help us be more effective in sharing the gospel. We can pray for those we witness to, asking God to open their hearts and protect them from spiritual opposition. We can also seek to present the gospel in ways that are clear, relevant, and engaging, addressing the cultural and personal barriers they may face.

2. Teaching and Preaching: For those involved in teaching and preaching, understanding the dynamics of spiritual receptivity can inform how we communicate God's word. We can strive to make our messages clear and accessible, using illustrations and explanations that resonate with our audience. Additionally, we can emphasize the importance of personal application and encourage our listeners to reflect on how the teachings apply to their lives.

3. Personal Spiritual Development: On a personal level, understanding the need for spiritual receptivity can motivate us to cultivate practices that foster growth. This includes regular engagement with scripture, prayer, and participation in community. Recognizing the reality of spiritual opposition can also prompt us to be vigilant in guarding our hearts and minds, seeking to remain grounded in God's truth.

4. Support for New Believers: Supporting new believers in their faith journey is crucial, as they may be particularly vulnerable to the tactics of the evil one. Providing discipleship and mentorship, creating a supportive community, and helping them develop spiritual disciplines can strengthen their understanding and resilience.

The Importance of Continual Learning

Jesus' explanation of the wayside also underscores the importance of continual learning and growth in our spiritual journey. Spiritual understanding is not a one-time achievement but an ongoing process that requires dedication and intentionality.

1. Ongoing Engagement with Scripture: Continual engagement with scripture is essential for deepening our understanding of God's word. This involves reading, studying, meditating, and applying the Bible regularly. As we grow in our knowledge of scripture, we can develop a deeper appreciation for its richness and relevance.

2. Lifelong Learning: Spiritual growth involves a commitment to lifelong learning. This means being open to new insights, seeking wisdom from others, and being willing to adapt and grow. Whether through formal education, personal study, or conversations with fellow believers, we can continue to expand our understanding of God's truth.

3. Reflective Practice: Reflective practice is a valuable tool for spiritual growth. This involves regularly examining our thoughts, attitudes, and behaviors in light of scripture, seeking to align our lives with God's will. Reflection can help us identify areas where we need to grow and make intentional changes.

4. Seeking Guidance from the Holy Spirit: The Holy Spirit plays a crucial role in guiding us into all truth. Continually seeking the Spirit's guidance through prayer and openness to His leading can help us grow in our understanding and application of God's word.

The Role of the Church in Fostering Understanding

The church has a vital role in fostering spiritual understanding and supporting believers in their faith journey. As a community of faith, the church can create an environment that encourages growth, learning, and resilience.

1. Teaching and Preaching: The church's teaching and preaching ministry is central to fostering understanding. By providing sound biblical teaching, pastors and teachers can help congregants grasp the truths of scripture and apply them to their lives. Expository preaching, which involves explaining and applying the text, can be particularly effective in deepening understanding.

2. Discipleship Programs: Discipleship programs can provide structured opportunities for growth and learning. These programs can include Bible studies, small groups, mentorship, and classes that cover various aspects of the Christian faith. By participating in discipleship programs, believers can develop a strong foundation and grow in their understanding of God's word.

3. Community and Fellowship: The church community provides a context for mutual support and encouragement. Through fellowship, believers can share their experiences, offer insights, and pray for one another. This communal aspect of faith is vital for spiritual growth and resilience.

4. Prayer and Intercession: The church can also play a role in interceding for its members, asking God to open hearts and minds to His truth. Corporate prayer and intercession can create a supportive environment where individuals are uplifted and strengthened in their faith.

5. Resources and Opportunities: Providing resources and opportunities for growth is another way the church can support spiritual understanding. This can

include offering books, study guides, and online resources, as well as organizing workshops, retreats, and conferences that focus on spiritual development.

Conclusion

Jesus' explanation of the wayside in the parable of the sower provides profound insights into the dynamics of spiritual understanding and the challenges that prevent it. The seeds that fall by the wayside represent those who hear the message of the Kingdom but do not understand it, with the evil one actively working to snatch away what was sown.

Understanding the nature of spiritual receptivity, the obstacles to comprehension, and the role of the evil one can inform our approach to evangelism, teaching, and personal spiritual growth. By cultivating a receptive heart, engaging with scripture, and remaining vigilant against spiritual opposition, we can deepen our understanding and experience the transformative power of God's word.

The broader implications for discipleship and spiritual growth highlight the importance of continual learning, community support, and the church's role in fostering understanding. As we seek to grow in our faith, let us be mindful of the need for humility, teachability, and a reliance on the Holy Spirit.

In our journey of faith, may we strive to cultivate hearts that are open and receptive to God's truth, allowing His word to take root and bear fruit in our lives. Let us be vigilant in guarding against the tactics of the evil one, and let us support one another in our shared pursuit of spiritual growth and understanding.

Chapter 12: The Explanation of the Stony Ground

Summary: Jesus explains that the seeds on stony ground represent those who hear the word and receive it with joy, but they have no root and fall away when trouble comes.

Bible Verse: Matthew 13:20-21

As the evening light faded, casting long shadows across the landscape, Jesus continued to impart deeper spiritual truths to His disciples. He had spoken in parables to the multitudes, but now He was providing His closest followers with detailed explanations. The parable of the sower was one such story, rich with meaning and insight into the human heart's response to God's word.

Jesus said, "The seed falling on rocky ground refers to someone who hears the word and at once receives it with joy. But since they have no root, they last only a short time. When trouble or persecution comes because of the word, they quickly fall away" (Matthew 13:20-21).

In this chapter, we will delve into Jesus' explanation of the stony ground in the parable of the sower. We will explore the characteristics of this type of soil, the reasons for the initial enthusiastic response, the lack of deep roots, and the consequences of falling away under pressure. Additionally, we will consider practical applications for developing a deep and resilient faith and the broader implications for discipleship and spiritual growth.

Characteristics of the Stony Ground

The stony ground, as described by Jesus, represents a type of heart that initially responds to God's word with joy but lacks the depth necessary for sustained growth and endurance. To understand this type of soil, we need to examine its characteristics and the factors that contribute to its superficiality.

1. Superficial Receptivity: The stony ground is characterized by a thin layer of soil covering a bedrock of stone. This superficial layer allows the seed to germinate quickly, leading to an immediate and enthusiastic response. However, the lack of depth prevents the seed from developing strong roots, making it vulnerable to adverse conditions.

2. Lack of Depth: The primary issue with the stony ground is its lack of depth. There is not enough soil for the roots to penetrate deeply, which means the plant cannot access the necessary nutrients and water for sustained growth. This shallow foundation makes the plant susceptible to environmental stressors.

3. Initial Enthusiasm: The seed on stony ground represents individuals who hear the word and receive it with joy. This initial enthusiasm is genuine and often marked by an emotional response. The message of the Kingdom resonates with them, and they are eager to embrace it.

4. Vulnerability to Adversity: Despite the initial positive response, the lack of deep roots makes these individuals vulnerable to adversity. When trouble or persecution arises because of the word, they quickly fall away. The superficiality of their faith cannot withstand the pressures and challenges they encounter.

Reasons for Initial Enthusiastic Response

The initial enthusiastic response to God's word is a significant aspect of the stony ground. Understanding the reasons behind this response can provide insight into the nature of superficial faith and the factors that contribute to its fragility.

1. Emotional Appeal: The message of the Kingdom can evoke strong emotions, such as joy, hope, and excitement. The promise of salvation, forgiveness, and eternal life resonates deeply with individuals, leading to an enthusiastic reception. This emotional appeal can be a powerful motivator for an initial response.

2. Personal Needs and Desires: Individuals may be drawn to the gospel because it addresses their personal needs and desires. The offer of healing, peace, and purpose can be compelling, especially for those experiencing brokenness, anxiety, or a sense of meaninglessness. The gospel provides answers to their deepest longings.

3. Social and Cultural Influence: Social and cultural factors can also play a role in the initial enthusiastic response. The influence of friends, family, or a faith community can encourage individuals to embrace the gospel. Cultural trends and movements that emphasize spirituality or religious revival can create an environment conducive to an enthusiastic reception.

4. Immediate Benefits: The immediate benefits of faith, such as a sense of belonging, community support, and positive changes in behavior and outlook, can contribute to the initial response. These benefits can create a sense of fulfillment and satisfaction, reinforcing the enthusiastic reception of the gospel.

The Lack of Deep Roots

While the initial response to God's word is positive, the lack of deep roots is a critical issue for those represented by the stony ground. This lack of depth prevents sustained growth and makes individuals susceptible to falling away under pressure. Understanding the reasons for this lack of deep roots can help us address the challenges of superficial faith.

1. Shallow Engagement with Scripture: One of the primary reasons for the lack of deep roots is shallow engagement with scripture. Individuals may read the Bible sporadically or superficially, without delving deeply into its meaning and application. This superficial engagement limits their understanding and prevents the development of a strong foundation.

2. Inadequate Discipleship: Effective discipleship is essential for spiritual growth and resilience. Without proper guidance, mentoring, and teaching, individuals may struggle to develop a deep and robust faith. Inadequate discipleship leaves them vulnerable to doubts, misconceptions, and external pressures.

3. Neglect of Spiritual Disciplines: Spiritual disciplines such as prayer, meditation, fasting, and fellowship are vital for deepening one's relationship with God. Neglecting these practices can result in a weak and shallow faith. Consistent engagement in spiritual disciplines fosters spiritual maturity and resilience.

4. Unresolved Sin and Inner Struggles: Unresolved sin and inner struggles can hinder the development of deep roots. Guilt, shame, and ongoing sinful behavior can create barriers to spiritual growth. Addressing these issues through confession, repentance, and seeking God's grace is essential for cultivating a deep and resilient faith.

5. External Pressures and Distractions: The pressures and distractions of life, such as work, relationships, and societal expectations, can divert attention from spiritual growth. These external factors can consume time and energy,

leaving little room for deepening one's faith. Prioritizing spiritual growth amidst these pressures is crucial.

Consequences of Falling Away Under Pressure

The superficiality of faith represented by the stony ground leads to significant consequences when individuals face trouble or persecution. Understanding these consequences can highlight the importance of developing a deep and resilient faith.

1. Spiritual Discouragement: Falling away under pressure can lead to spiritual discouragement and disillusionment. The initial enthusiasm fades, and individuals may feel abandoned by God or question the validity of their faith. This discouragement can result in a loss of hope and motivation to continue in the faith journey.

2. Loss of Witness: When individuals fall away, their witness to others is compromised. The testimony of their faith becomes inconsistent, and their credibility is undermined. This loss of witness can impact the faith of others and hinder the spread of the gospel.

3. Missed Opportunities for Growth: Falling away prevents individuals from experiencing the transformative growth that comes from enduring trials and challenges. Perseverance through adversity leads to spiritual maturity, character development, and a deeper relationship with God. Missing these opportunities stunts spiritual growth.

4. Separation from Community: Falling away can result in separation from the faith community. The support, encouragement, and accountability provided by fellow believers are essential for spiritual growth and resilience. Isolation from the community can lead to further spiritual decline and vulnerability.

5. Eternal Implications: The ultimate consequence of falling away is the potential loss of eternal life. Persisting in faith is essential for salvation, and falling away indicates a failure to remain steadfast in the commitment to follow Christ. This sobering reality underscores the urgency of cultivating a deep and resilient faith.

Practical Applications for Developing a Deep and

Resilient Faith

Given the challenges of superficial faith and the consequences of falling away, it is essential to develop a deep and resilient faith. Here are several practical steps to foster spiritual depth and resilience.

1. Regular and Intentional Engagement with Scripture: Consistent and intentional engagement with scripture is vital for spiritual growth. This involves not only reading the Bible but also studying its context, meditating on its truths, and applying its teachings to daily life. Developing a habit of daily Bible reading and study can deepen one's understanding and strengthen faith.

2. Commitment to Spiritual Disciplines: Engaging in spiritual disciplines such as prayer, fasting, meditation, and fellowship is crucial for developing a resilient faith. These practices foster intimacy with God, provide spiritual nourishment, and build spiritual strength. Regular participation in these disciplines creates a strong foundation for enduring trials.

3. Seeking Effective Discipleship: Effective discipleship is essential for spiritual growth. This involves seeking guidance from mature believers, participating in discipleship programs, and being open to mentoring relationships. Discipleship provides accountability, encouragement, and practical wisdom for navigating the challenges of faith.

4. Addressing Sin and Inner Struggles: Confronting and addressing sin and inner struggles is critical for cultivating a deep faith. This involves confession, repentance, and seeking God's forgiveness and grace. Overcoming these barriers allows for spiritual healing and growth.

5. Prioritizing Spiritual Growth Amidst External Pressures: Navigating the pressures and distractions of life requires intentional prioritization of spiritual growth. Setting aside dedicated time for spiritual practices, creating boundaries to protect this time, and seeking balance in life can help maintain focus on spiritual development.

6. Building a Supportive Community: Being part of a supportive faith community provides essential support, encouragement, and accountability. Participating in small groups, Bible studies, and church activities fosters relationships with fellow believers who can offer insights, prayer, and mutual support.

7. Embracing Trials as Opportunities for Growth: Viewing trials and challenges as opportunities for growth can transform the way we respond to adversity. Persevering through difficulties with faith and trust in God leads to spiritual maturity and a deeper relationship with Him.

Embracing trials as part of the faith journey builds resilience.

Broader Implications for Discipleship and Spiritual Growth

Jesus' explanation of the stony ground has broader implications for discipleship and spiritual growth. Understanding the dynamics of superficial faith and the importance of deep roots can inform our approach to teaching, mentoring, and supporting others in their faith journey.

1. Teaching and Preaching: In teaching and preaching, it is important to address the need for deep spiritual roots. Providing sound biblical teaching, emphasizing the importance of spiritual disciplines, and encouraging personal application can help individuals develop a resilient faith. Addressing the challenges of superficial faith and offering practical guidance can equip believers to endure trials.

2. Discipleship and Mentorship: Effective discipleship and mentorship are crucial for fostering spiritual growth. This involves walking alongside individuals, providing guidance, encouragement, and accountability. Mentors can help identify areas of shallow faith and offer practical steps for deepening one's relationship with God.

3. Creating a Supportive Community: Building a supportive faith community is essential for spiritual resilience. Creating an environment where individuals feel valued, supported, and encouraged fosters spiritual growth. Providing opportunities for fellowship, small group participation, and communal worship strengthens the bonds within the community and promotes mutual support.

4. Encouraging Lifelong Learning: Emphasizing the importance of lifelong learning in the faith journey can inspire individuals to continually seek spiritual growth. Encouraging engagement with scripture, participation in educational programs, and openness to new insights fosters a culture of growth and resilience within the church.

5. Addressing the Reality of Spiritual Warfare: Recognizing and addressing the reality of spiritual warfare is crucial for supporting believers in their faith journey. Teaching about the tactics of the evil one, providing tools for spiritual discernment, and emphasizing the importance of spiritual armor can equip individuals to stand firm in the face of opposition.

Conclusion

Jesus' explanation of the stony ground in the parable of the sower provides profound insights into the dynamics of superficial faith and the challenges of developing deep spiritual roots. The seeds that fall on stony ground represent those who hear the word and receive it with joy but have no root and fall away when trouble comes.

Understanding the characteristics of the stony ground, the reasons for the initial enthusiastic response, the lack of deep roots, and the consequences of falling away can inform our approach to spiritual growth and discipleship. By cultivating a deep and resilient faith through regular engagement with scripture, commitment to spiritual disciplines, effective discipleship, addressing sin and inner struggles, prioritizing spiritual growth amidst external pressures, building a supportive community, and embracing trials as opportunities for growth, we can develop a faith that endures.

The broader implications for teaching, mentoring, and supporting others in their faith journey highlight the importance of fostering spiritual depth and resilience within the church community. As we seek to grow in our faith and support others in their journey, let us strive to cultivate hearts that are deeply rooted in God's word, able to withstand the trials and challenges of life, and bear fruit for the Kingdom of Heaven.

Chapter 13: The Explanation of the Thorns

Summary: Jesus explains that the seeds among thorns represent those who hear the word, but the worries of this life and the deceitfulness of wealth choke it, making it unfruitful.

Bible Verse: Matthew 13:22

As the night descended and the stars began to appear in the sky, Jesus continued to reveal the deeper meanings of His parables to His disciples. Among the many parables He shared, the parable of the sower stood out for its rich metaphors and profound insights into the human response to God's word. Jesus explained that the seeds sown among thorns represent those who hear the word, but the worries of this life and the deceitfulness of wealth choke it, making it unfruitful.

In Matthew 13:22, Jesus said, "The seed falling among the thorns refers to someone who hears the word, but the worries of this life and the deceitfulness of wealth choke the word, making it unfruitful."

This chapter will delve into Jesus' explanation of the thorns in the parable of the sower. We will explore the nature of the thorns, the impact of life's worries and wealth's deceitfulness on spiritual growth, and practical applications for cultivating a fruitful faith. Additionally, we will consider the broader implications for discipleship, spiritual growth, and community support.

The Nature of the Thorns

In the parable of the sower, the thorns represent various factors that hinder the growth and fruitfulness of the word of God in an individual's life. To understand this metaphor, we need to examine the characteristics of the thorns and how they relate to the spiritual challenges faced by believers.

1. Competition for Resources: Thorns compete with the good plants for essential resources such as sunlight, water, and nutrients. This competition hinders the growth of the good plants, preventing them from reaching their full potential. Spiritually, this represents the distractions and competing priorities that draw individuals away from focusing on God's word and living according to His will.

2. Invasive Growth: Thorns have an invasive nature, spreading quickly and entangling themselves around other plants. This invasive growth chokes the life out of the good plants, making them unfruitful. In the spiritual realm, this symbolizes the pervasive influence of worries and wealth, which can dominate an individual's thoughts and actions, crowding out the transformative power of the gospel.

3. Hidden Dangers: Thorns often grow unnoticed until they have already established themselves firmly in the soil. By the time their presence is fully recognized, they have already caused significant damage. Similarly, the worries of life and the deceitfulness of wealth can subtly infiltrate an individual's heart and mind, gradually diminishing their spiritual vitality without immediate awareness.

4. Resilience and Persistence: Thorns are resilient and difficult to eradicate. Even after being cut down, they often grow back, requiring constant vigilance and effort to keep them under control. This persistence mirrors the ongoing challenges of dealing with life's worries and the temptations of wealth, which require continuous attention and intentionality to manage effectively.

The Impact of Life's Worries

Jesus identified the worries of this life as one of the key factors that choke the word of God, making it unfruitful. To understand the full impact of these worries, we need to explore their nature, sources, and effects on spiritual growth.

1. Nature of Worries: Worries are often characterized by anxiety, fear, and a sense of uncertainty about the future. They can stem from various aspects of life, including health, finances, relationships, career, and personal well-being. These concerns can consume an individual's thoughts and emotions, leading to a preoccupation with potential problems and challenges.

2. Sources of Worries: The sources of worries are diverse and can vary from person to person. Common sources include:

- Financial Concerns: Uncertainty about financial stability, debt, job security, and the ability to provide for oneself and one's family can lead to significant anxiety.

- Health Issues: Concerns about personal health, the well-being of loved ones, and potential medical problems can create ongoing stress and fear.

- Relationship Struggles: Conflicts, misunderstandings, and fears about the stability of relationships with family, friends, and significant others can contribute to emotional turmoil.

- Work and Career Pressures: Job-related stress, fear of failure, and concerns about career advancement can dominate an individual's thoughts and energy.

- Future Uncertainty: General uncertainty about the future, including fears about societal changes, environmental issues, and global events, can lead to pervasive anxiety.

3. Effects on Spiritual Growth: The worries of life can have several detrimental effects on spiritual growth:

- Distraction from God's Word: Worries can divert attention away from engaging with scripture, prayer, and other spiritual disciplines. The constant preoccupation with problems and anxieties can make it difficult to focus on God's promises and guidance.

- Erosion of Trust in God: Persistent worries can undermine trust in God's provision and sovereignty. When individuals become fixated on their concerns, they may struggle to believe that God is in control and capable of addressing their needs.

- Impaired Spiritual Discernment: Anxiety and fear can cloud judgment and spiritual discernment, making it challenging to perceive God's will and direction. The noise of worries can drown out the still, small voice of the Holy Spirit.

- Diminished Joy and Peace: The peace and joy that come from a close relationship with God can be overshadowed by the constant presence of worries. This emotional burden can hinder the experience of the abundant life that Jesus promised.

The Deceitfulness of Wealth

In addition to the worries of life, Jesus identified the deceitfulness of wealth as another factor that chokes the word of God. To understand this aspect, we need to explore the nature of wealth's deceitfulness, its allure, and its impact on spiritual growth.

1. Nature of Wealth's Deceitfulness: Wealth is deceitful because it creates a false sense of security, satisfaction, and identity. It promises fulfillment and happiness but often leads to disillusionment and spiritual emptiness. The pursuit of wealth can become an idol, taking the place of God in an individual's life.

2. Allure of Wealth: Wealth has a powerful allure, offering the promise of comfort, status, and control. The desire for financial success and material possessions can become a driving force, shaping an individual's priorities and decisions. This allure is reinforced by societal values that equate wealth with success and worth.

3. Impact on Spiritual Growth: The deceitfulness of wealth can have several adverse effects on spiritual growth:

- Displacement of God:The pursuit of wealth can displace God as the primary focus and source of security. When individuals place their trust in money and material possessions, they may neglect their relationship with God and fail to seek His guidance and provision.

- Compromise of Values: The desire for wealth can lead to ethical compromises and decisions that are contrary to God's will. The temptation to cut corners, engage in dishonest practices, or prioritize financial gain over integrity can erode spiritual character.

- Diversion of Resources: The accumulation of wealth can divert resources away from serving God's purposes and helping others. Instead of using their blessings to advance the Kingdom and support those in need, individuals may hoard their wealth for personal gratification.

- False Sense of Independence: Wealth can create a false sense of independence and self-sufficiency, leading individuals to rely on their abilities and resources rather than depending on God. This attitude can hinder humility and openness to God's guidance.

Practical Applications for Cultivating a Fruitful Faith

Given the challenges posed by the worries of life and the deceitfulness of wealth, it is essential to cultivate a faith that is resilient and fruitful. Here are several practical steps to foster spiritual growth and overcome the obstacles represented by the thorns.

1. Prioritizing God's Word: Making the study and meditation of God's word a priority is crucial for spiritual growth. This involves setting aside dedicated time for reading the Bible, reflecting on its teachings, and applying its principles to daily life. Regular engagement with scripture helps to anchor faith and provides guidance for navigating life's challenges.

2. Developing a Prayerful Life: Cultivating a consistent and meaningful prayer life is essential for maintaining a close relationship with God. Prayer provides a channel for expressing concerns, seeking God's guidance, and experiencing His peace. Regular communication with God helps to alleviate worries and reinforce trust in His provision.

3. Practicing Contentment: Embracing a mindset of contentment and gratitude can counteract the deceitfulness of wealth. Recognizing and appreciating God's blessings, both material and spiritual, fosters a sense of fulfillment and reduces the desire for more. Contentment shifts the focus from accumulation to stewardship and generosity.

4. Engaging in Generous Giving: Practicing generosity and giving to others can break the hold of materialism and wealth's deceitfulness. By sharing resources and supporting those in need, individuals can demonstrate trust in God's provision and align their values with His Kingdom. Generous giving reflects God's character and advances His purposes.

5. Seeking Community Support: Being part of a faith community provides essential support and accountability. Fellowship with other believers offers encouragement, prayer, and practical assistance in dealing with life's worries and challenges. Small groups, Bible studies, and church activities foster relationships that strengthen faith and provide mutual support.

6. Embracing Simplicity: Adopting a lifestyle of simplicity can help to reduce the distractions and pressures associated with wealth and materialism. Simplifying one's life involves evaluating priorities, decluttering possessions, and focusing on what truly matters. This approach creates space for spiritual growth and reduces the influence of wealth's deceitfulness.

7. Trusting in God's Provision: Developing a deep trust in God's provision and sovereignty is essential for overcoming the worries of life. This involves believing that God is in control and capable of meeting all needs. Trust is

cultivated through prayer, reflection on God's faithfulness, and relying on His promises.

8. Cultivating a Kingdom Perspective: Adopting a Kingdom perspective helps to prioritize spiritual growth and eternal values over temporal concerns. This perspective involves seeking first the Kingdom of God and His righteousness (Matthew 6:33), recognizing that true fulfillment and security are found in Him. A Kingdom perspective shifts focus from worldly worries and wealth to God's purposes and promises.

Broader Implications for Discipleship and Spiritual Growth

Jesus' explanation of the thorns has broader implications for discipleship and spiritual growth. Understanding the dynamics of the worries of life and the deceitfulness of wealth can inform our approach to teaching, mentoring, and supporting others in their faith journey.

1. Teaching and Preaching:** In teaching and preaching, it is important to address the challenges of life's worries and wealth's deceitfulness. Providing sound biblical teaching on these topics, emphasizing the importance of trust in God, and offering practical guidance for dealing with these challenges can equip individuals to navigate their faith journey effectively.

2. Discipleship and Mentorship: Effective discipleship and mentorship involve addressing the specific challenges faced by individuals. Mentors can help identify the influence of worries and wealth in their mentees' lives and offer personalized guidance and support. Encouraging spiritual disciplines, providing accountability, and sharing personal experiences can strengthen resilience and faith.

3. Creating a Supportive Community: Building a supportive faith community is essential for fostering spiritual growth. Creating an environment where individuals feel valued, supported, and encouraged fosters spiritual growth. Providing opportunities for fellowship, small group participation, and communal worship strengthens the bonds within the community and promotes mutual support.

4. Encouraging Lifelong Learning: Emphasizing the importance of lifelong learning in the faith journey can inspire individuals to continually seek spiritual

growth. Encouraging engagement with scripture, participation in educational programs, and openness to new insights fosters a culture of growth and resilience within the church.

5. Addressing the Reality of Spiritual Warfare: Recognizing and addressing the reality of spiritual warfare is crucial for supporting believers in their faith journey. Teaching about the tactics of the evil one, providing tools for spiritual discernment, and emphasizing the importance of spiritual armor can equip individuals to stand firm in the face of opposition.

Conclusion

Jesus' explanation of the thorns in the parable of the sower provides profound insights into the dynamics of spiritual growth and the challenges that can hinder fruitfulness. The seeds that fall among the thorns represent those who hear the word, but the worries of this life and the deceitfulness of wealth choke it, making it unfruitful.

Understanding the nature of the thorns, the impact of life's worries, and the deceitfulness of wealth can inform our approach to spiritual growth and discipleship. By prioritizing God's word, developing a prayerful life, practicing contentment, engaging in generous giving, seeking community support, embracing simplicity, trusting in God's provision, and cultivating a Kingdom perspective, we can develop a fruitful faith that withstands the challenges of life.

The broader implications for teaching, mentoring, and supporting others in their faith journey highlight the importance of fostering spiritual depth and resilience within the church community. As we seek to grow in our faith and support others in their journey, let us strive to cultivate hearts that are free from the thorns of worries and wealth, able to bear fruit for the Kingdom of Heaven.

Chapter 14: The Explanation of the Good Ground

Summary: Jesus explains that the seeds on good ground represent those who hear the word, understand it, and produce a crop yielding a hundred, sixty, or thirty times what was sown.

Bible Verse: Matthew 13:23

As the night deepened and the stars filled the sky, Jesus continued to reveal the depths of His teachings to His disciples. Among the many lessons He shared, the parable of the sower held profound significance, illustrating the varied responses to the word of God. In this intimate setting, Jesus explained the meaning of the good ground, providing a powerful vision of fruitful discipleship.

Jesus said, "But the seed falling on good soil refers to someone who hears the word and understands it. This is the one who produces a crop, yielding a hundred, sixty or thirty times what was sown" (Matthew 13:23).

In this chapter, we will explore Jesus' explanation of the good ground in the parable of the sower. We will examine the characteristics of the good ground, the process of hearing and understanding the word, the nature of spiritual fruitfulness, and practical applications for cultivating a productive faith. Additionally, we will consider the broader implications for discipleship, spiritual growth, and community impact.

Characteristics of the Good Ground

The good ground in the parable of the sower represents the heart that is open, receptive, and prepared to receive the word of God. To understand this metaphor, we need to explore the characteristics that define good ground and how they relate to a fruitful spiritual life.

1. Receptivity and Openness: Good ground is characterized by its receptivity to the seed. It is free from the obstacles that hinder growth, such as hard paths, rocks, and thorns. Spiritually, this represents a heart that is open to God's word, willing to receive and respond to His teachings. An open heart is

free from pride, resistance, and distractions, creating a fertile environment for the seed to take root.

2. Depth and Preparation: Good ground is well-prepared, with sufficient depth to allow roots to grow deeply. This preparation involves removing rocks and weeds, breaking up hard soil, and ensuring that the soil is nutrient-rich. Spiritually, this represents a heart that is prepared through spiritual disciplines, such as prayer, study of scripture, and repentance. A well-prepared heart has the depth and capacity to nurture and sustain the word of God.

3. Nutrient-Rich Environment: Good ground provides the necessary nutrients for the seed to grow and flourish. This includes adequate water, sunlight, and minerals. Spiritually, this represents a life that is nourished by the Holy Spirit, fellowship with other believers, and engagement with God's word. A nutrient-rich environment supports continuous growth and development.

4. Freedom from Hindrances: Good ground is free from hindrances that can impede growth. This includes removing weeds, thorns, and anything that can choke the life out of the seed. Spiritually, this represents a life that is free from sin, distractions, and worldly concerns that can divert attention from God's word. A life free from hindrances allows for uninterrupted growth and fruitfulness.

The Process of Hearing and Understanding the Word

Jesus emphasized that those who represent the good ground are those who hear the word and understand it. To explore this process, we need to examine the steps involved in truly hearing and understanding God's word and how this leads to spiritual fruitfulness.

1. Attentive Listening: The first step in the process is attentive listening. This involves being fully present and engaged when hearing the word of God. Attentive listening requires setting aside distractions and focusing on the message being conveyed. This can happen in various contexts, such as during personal Bible study, sermons, or conversations with fellow believers.

2. Reflective Meditation: After hearing the word, the next step is reflective meditation. This involves pondering the message, considering its implications, and seeking to understand its deeper meaning. Reflective meditation allows individuals to internalize the word and apply it to their lives. This step is

crucial for moving beyond mere intellectual understanding to heart-level comprehension.

3. Prayerful Consideration: Prayerful consideration is an essential part of understanding God's word. This involves seeking the guidance of the Holy Spirit to illuminate the scriptures and reveal their relevance. Prayerful consideration invites God's presence into the process, allowing for divine insight and wisdom. It is through prayer that individuals can discern God's will and direction.

4. Intentional Application: Understanding the word of God must lead to intentional application. This involves putting the teachings into practice and allowing them to shape one's thoughts, actions, and decisions. Intentional application is where true transformation occurs, as individuals align their lives with God's principles and values.

5. Ongoing Reflection and Growth: The process of hearing and understanding the word is ongoing. Continuous reflection and growth are necessary for sustained spiritual development. This involves regularly revisiting the scriptures, seeking new insights, and making adjustments as needed. Ongoing reflection ensures that the word remains active and influential in one's life.

The Nature of Spiritual Fruitfulness

Jesus described the good ground as producing a crop yielding a hundred, sixty, or thirty times what was sown. To understand the nature of spiritual fruitfulness, we need to explore what it means to bear fruit and how this fruitfulness manifests in the life of a believer.

1. Transformation of Character: Spiritual fruitfulness involves the transformation of character, evidenced by the fruit of the Spirit. Galatians 5:22-23 describes the fruit of the Spirit as love, joy, peace, forbearance, kindness, goodness, faithfulness, gentleness, and self-control. These qualities reflect the character of Christ and are the result of the Holy Spirit's work in a believer's life.

2. Impact on Others: Spiritual fruitfulness extends beyond personal transformation to impact others. This includes sharing the gospel, serving those in need, and living out the principles of the Kingdom in everyday interactions.

A fruitful life influences others positively, drawing them closer to God and encouraging them in their faith journey.

3. Advancement of God's Kingdom: Spiritual fruitfulness contributes to the advancement of God's Kingdom. This involves participating in God's redemptive work, whether through evangelism, discipleship, social justice, or other forms of ministry. Fruitful believers play a vital role in expanding the reach of the gospel and making a tangible difference in the world.

4. Perseverance and Endurance: Spiritual fruitfulness requires perseverance and endurance. The process of bearing fruit is ongoing and involves facing challenges, trials, and opposition. Fruitful believers remain steadfast in their faith, trusting in God's provision and guidance. Perseverance ensures that the fruit produced is lasting and impactful.

5. Multiplication of Efforts: Spiritual fruitfulness is characterized by the multiplication of efforts. Just as a single seed can produce multiple fruits, a fruitful believer's efforts can lead to exponential growth and influence. This multiplication can happen through mentoring, teaching, and inspiring others to live fruitful lives. The impact of a fruitful believer can extend far beyond their immediate context.

Practical Applications for Cultivating a Productive Faith

Given the importance of good ground for spiritual fruitfulness, it is essential to cultivate a faith that is productive and resilient. Here are several practical steps to foster spiritual growth and ensure that one's life is good ground for God's word.

1. Regular Engagement with Scripture: Consistent engagement with scripture is foundational for spiritual growth. This involves reading, studying, meditating on, and applying the Bible regularly. Developing a habit of daily Bible reading and study can deepen understanding and strengthen faith.

2. Commitment to Spiritual Disciplines: Engaging in spiritual disciplines such as prayer, fasting, meditation, and worship is crucial for nurturing a productive faith. These practices foster intimacy with God, provide spiritual nourishment, and build spiritual strength. Regular participation in these disciplines creates a strong foundation for enduring trials and bearing fruit.

3. Seeking Effective Discipleship: Effective discipleship is essential for spiritual growth. This involves seeking guidance from mature believers, participating in discipleship programs, and being open to mentoring relationships. Discipleship provides accountability, encouragement, and practical wisdom for navigating the challenges of faith.

4. Addressing Sin and Inner Struggles: Confronting and addressing sin and inner struggles is critical for cultivating a productive faith. This involves confession, repentance, and seeking God's forgiveness and grace. Overcoming these barriers allows for spiritual healing and growth.

5. Prioritizing Spiritual Growth Amidst External Pressures: Navigating the pressures and distractions of life requires intentional prioritization of spiritual growth. Setting aside dedicated time for spiritual practices, creating boundaries to protect this time, and seeking balance in life can help maintain focus on spiritual development.

6. Building a Supportive Community: Being part of a supportive faith community provides essential support, encouragement, and accountability. Participating in small groups, Bible studies, and church activities fosters relationships with fellow believers who can offer insights, prayer, and mutual support.

7. Embracing Trials as Opportunities for Growth: Viewing trials and challenges as opportunities for growth can transform the way we respond to adversity. Persevering through difficulties with faith and trust in God leads to spiritual maturity and a deeper relationship with Him. Embracing trials as part of the faith journey builds resilience and fruitfulness.

8. Cultivating a Kingdom Perspective: Adopting a Kingdom perspective helps to prioritize spiritual growth and eternal values over temporal concerns. This perspective involves seeking first the Kingdom of God and His righteousness (Matthew 6:33), recognizing that true fulfillment and security are found in Him. A Kingdom perspective shifts focus from worldly worries and wealth to God's purposes and promises.

The Broader Implications for Discipleship and Spiritual Growth

Jesus' explanation of the good ground has broader implications for discipleship and spiritual growth. Understanding the dynamics of spiritual fruitfulness can inform our approach to teaching, mentoring, and supporting others in their faith journey.

1. Teaching and Preaching: In teaching and preaching, it is important to emphasize the characteristics of good ground and the process of spiritual fruitfulness. Providing sound biblical teaching on these topics, emphasizing the importance of a receptive heart, and offering practical guidance for cultivating a productive faith can equip individuals to navigate their faith journey effectively.

2. Discipleship and Mentorship: Effective discipleship and mentorship involve guiding individuals through the process of hearing, understanding, and applying God's word. Mentors can help identify areas of growth, offer personalized guidance and support, and encourage spiritual disciplines. Discipleship relationships provide accountability and encouragement, fostering spiritual resilience and fruitfulness.

3. Creating a Supportive Community: Building a supportive faith community is essential for fostering spiritual growth. Creating an environment where individuals feel valued, supported, and encouraged fosters spiritual growth. Providing opportunities for fellowship, small group participation, and communal worship strengthens the bonds within the community and promotes mutual support.

4. Encouraging Lifelong Learning: Emphasizing the importance of lifelong learning in the faith journey can inspire individuals to continually seek spiritual growth. Encouraging engagement with scripture, participation in educational programs, and openness to new insights fosters a culture of growth and resilience within the church.

5. Addressing the Reality of Spiritual Warfare: Recognizing and addressing the reality of spiritual warfare is crucial for supporting believers in their faith journey. Teaching about the tactics of the evil one, providing tools for spiritual discernment, and emphasizing the importance of spiritual armor can equip individuals to stand firm in the face of opposition.

Conclusion

Jesus' explanation of the good ground in the parable of the sower provides profound insights into the dynamics of spiritual growth and the characteristics of a fruitful faith. The seeds that fall on good ground represent those who hear the word, understand it, and produce a crop yielding a hundred, sixty, or thirty times what was sown.

Understanding the characteristics of the good ground, the process of hearing and understanding the word, and the nature of spiritual fruitfulness can inform our approach to spiritual growth and discipleship. By prioritizing regular engagement with scripture, commitment to spiritual disciplines, effective discipleship, addressing sin and inner struggles, prioritizing spiritual growth amidst external pressures, building a supportive community, embracing trials as opportunities for growth, and cultivating a Kingdom perspective, we can develop a faith that is productive and resilient.

The broader implications for teaching, mentoring, and supporting others in their faith journey highlight the importance of fostering spiritual depth and resilience within the church community. As we seek to grow in our faith and support others in their journey, let us strive to cultivate hearts that are good ground for God's word, able to bear fruit for the Kingdom of Heaven and make a lasting impact in the world.

Chapter 15: The Parable's Application

Summary: Reflections on how the parable applies to the lives of believers and the importance of cultivating a heart receptive to God's word.

Bible Verse: James 1:21

As Jesus concluded His teaching on the parable of the sower, He left His disciples with profound insights into the nature of spiritual receptivity and growth. The parable is not merely a story about agriculture; it is a powerful metaphor for understanding how the word of God interacts with different types of hearts. Reflecting on this parable, we can gain valuable lessons about cultivating a heart that is receptive to God's word and bearing fruit in our lives.

James 1:21 encapsulates the essence of this message: "Therefore, get rid of all moral filth and the evil that is so prevalent and humbly accept the word planted in you, which can save you." This verse calls believers to remove hindrances and humbly receive God's word, highlighting the importance of a receptive heart.

In this chapter, we will explore the practical applications of the parable of the sower for believers. We will delve into the significance of each type of soil, the process of cultivating a receptive heart, and the broader implications for discipleship and community life. By understanding how this parable applies to our lives, we can strive to be fruitful followers of Christ.

The Significance of Each Type of Soil

To fully appreciate the application of the parable of the sower, we need to revisit the significance of each type of soil and what it represents in the spiritual journey of a believer.

1. The Path (Hard Heart): The seed that falls on the path represents those who hear the word but do not understand it. The evil one quickly snatches away what was sown in their hearts. This type of soil signifies a hard heart, resistant to God's word. Hard-heartedness can stem from pride, unbelief, or a refusal to consider spiritual matters.

2. The Rocky Ground (Shallow Heart): The seed that falls on rocky ground represents those who hear the word and receive it with joy, but they have no

root. When trouble or persecution arises, they quickly fall away. This type of soil signifies a shallow heart, enthusiastic but lacking depth. Such individuals may be drawn to the emotional appeal of the gospel but fail to develop a strong, enduring faith.

3. The Thorns (Distracted Heart): The seed that falls among thorns represents those who hear the word, but the worries of this life and the deceitfulness of wealth choke it, making it unfruitful. This type of soil signifies a distracted heart, preoccupied with worldly concerns. The allure of wealth and the anxieties of life can overshadow the transformative power of the gospel.

4. The Good Ground (Receptive Heart): The seed that falls on good ground represents those who hear the word, understand it, and produce a crop yielding a hundred, sixty, or thirty times what was sown. This type of soil signifies a receptive heart, open and prepared to receive God's word. A receptive heart nurtures the seed, leading to spiritual growth and fruitfulness.

Cultivating a Receptive Heart

Cultivating a receptive heart is essential for experiencing the full impact of God's word and bearing fruit in our lives. This process involves several key steps that believers can take to ensure their hearts are good ground for the seed of God's word.

1. Self-Examination and Repentance: The first step in cultivating a receptive heart is self-examination and repentance. Believers must honestly assess the condition of their hearts, identifying areas of hardness, shallowness, or distraction. Repentance involves turning away from sin and seeking God's forgiveness and cleansing. This process prepares the heart to receive God's word.

2. Engaging with Scripture: Regular engagement with scripture is foundational for cultivating a receptive heart. This involves reading, studying, meditating on, and applying the Bible. Scripture provides the nourishment and guidance needed for spiritual growth. Believers should approach the Bible with humility, seeking to understand and apply its teachings.

3. Developing a Prayerful Life: Prayer is essential for maintaining a close relationship with God and cultivating a receptive heart. Through prayer, believers can seek God's guidance, express their concerns, and invite His

presence into their lives. Regular communication with God helps to align the heart with His will and fosters spiritual sensitivity.

4. Practicing Spiritual Disciplines: Spiritual disciplines such as fasting, meditation, worship, and fellowship play a crucial role in nurturing a receptive heart. These practices create space for God to work in the believer's life, promoting spiritual growth and resilience. Consistent participation in spiritual disciplines builds a strong foundation for faith.

5. Seeking Community and Accountability: Being part of a supportive faith community provides essential encouragement and accountability. Fellowship with other believers offers opportunities for mutual support, prayer, and growth. Small groups, Bible studies, and church activities foster relationships that strengthen faith and promote spiritual health.

6. Embracing Simplicity and Contentment: Simplifying one's life and practicing contentment can reduce the distractions and pressures associated with wealth and materialism. By focusing on what truly matters and being grateful for God's blessings, believers can create an environment conducive to spiritual growth. Contentment shifts the focus from accumulation to stewardship and generosity.

7. Trusting in God's Provision: Developing a deep trust in God's provision and sovereignty is crucial for overcoming the worries of life. Believers must trust that God is in control and capable of meeting all their needs. This trust is cultivated through prayer, reflection on God's faithfulness, and reliance on His promises.

8. Embracing Trials as Opportunities for Growth: Viewing trials and challenges as opportunities for growth can transform the way believers respond to adversity. Persevering through difficulties with faith and trust in God leads to spiritual maturity and a deeper relationship with Him. Embracing trials as part of the faith journey builds resilience and fruitfulness.

The Broader Implications for Discipleship and Community Life

The parable of the sower has broader implications for discipleship and community life. Understanding how to cultivate a receptive heart and bear fruit can inform our approach to teaching, mentoring, and supporting others in their faith journey.

1. Teaching and Preaching: In teaching and preaching, it is important to emphasize the characteristics of a receptive heart and the process of spiritual fruitfulness. Providing sound biblical teaching on these topics, emphasizing the importance of a receptive heart, and offering practical guidance for cultivating a productive faith can equip individuals to navigate their faith journey effectively.

2. Discipleship and Mentorship: Effective discipleship and mentorship involve guiding individuals through the process of hearing, understanding, and applying God's word. Mentors can help identify areas of growth, offer personalized guidance and support, and encourage spiritual disciplines. Discipleship relationships provide accountability and encouragement, fostering spiritual resilience and fruitfulness.

3. Creating a Supportive Community: Building a supportive faith community is essential for fostering spiritual growth. Creating an environment where individuals feel valued, supported, and encouraged fosters spiritual growth. Providing opportunities for fellowship, small group participation, and communal worship strengthens the bonds within the community and promotes mutual support.

4. Encouraging Lifelong Learning: Emphasizing the importance of lifelong learning in the faith journey can inspire individuals to continually seek spiritual growth. Encouraging engagement with scripture, participation in educational programs, and openness to new insights fosters a culture of growth and resilience within the church.

5. Addressing the Reality of Spiritual Warfare: Recognizing and addressing the reality of spiritual warfare is crucial for supporting believers in their faith journey. Teaching about the tactics of the evil one, providing tools for spiritual discernment, and emphasizing the importance of spiritual armor can equip individuals to stand firm in the face of opposition.

Practical Steps for Community Engagement and Support

To effectively apply the lessons of the parable of the sower within a community context, it is essential to implement practical steps that foster engagement and support. Here are several strategies that faith communities can adopt to cultivate receptive hearts and promote spiritual fruitfulness among their members.

1. Regular Bible Study and Discussion Groups: Organizing regular Bible study and discussion groups provides opportunities for members to engage deeply with scripture. These groups can foster a sense of community, encourage mutual support, and provide a platform for exploring the teachings of the Bible. Facilitators can guide discussions, offer insights, and create an environment where participants feel comfortable sharing their thoughts and questions.

2. Prayer Meetings and Spiritual Retreats: Hosting prayer meetings and spiritual retreats can strengthen the prayer life of the community and provide opportunities for reflection and renewal. These gatherings can help members develop a closer relationship with God and each other. Retreats, in particular, offer a dedicated time for spiritual growth, free from the distractions of daily life.

3. Mentorship and Discipleship Programs: Implementing mentorship and discipleship programs can provide personalized guidance and support for individuals at different stages of their faith journey. Pairing experienced believers with newer members can foster spiritual growth, accountability, and encouragement. These relationships can help mentees navigate challenges and deepen their understanding of God's word.

4. Service and Outreach Initiatives: Engaging in service and outreach initiatives allows members to put their faith into action and make a positive impact in their community. These activities can include volunteering at local shelters, organizing charity drives, or participating in mission trips. Serving others not only meets practical needs but also cultivates a heart of compassion and generosity.

5. Workshops and Seminars on Spiritual Disciplines: Offering workshops and seminars on spiritual disciplines such as prayer, fasting, meditation, and worship can provide practical tools for personal spiritual growth. These sessions can teach members how to incorporate these practices into their daily lives and highlight their importance for developing a receptive heart.

6. Creating a Culture of Encouragement and Accountability: Fostering a culture of encouragement and accountability within the community can promote spiritual resilience and fruitfulness. Encouraging members to share

their testimonies, celebrate each other's spiritual milestones, and hold one another accountable for their commitments can strengthen the bonds within the community and support individual growth.

7. Addressing Practical Concerns and Providing Resources: Recognizing and addressing the practical concerns of members, such as financial struggles, health issues, or relationship challenges, can help alleviate the worries that hinder spiritual growth. Providing resources, such as financial counseling, support groups, or access to professional services, can demonstrate the community's commitment to holistic well-being.

8. Promoting Lifelong Learning and Personal Development: Encouraging lifelong learning and personal development can inspire members to continually seek growth in their faith and other areas of life. This can include promoting educational opportunities, offering workshops on various topics, and encouraging members to pursue their interests and talents.

The Role of Leadership in Cultivating a Receptive Community

Leadership plays a crucial role in cultivating a receptive community and promoting spiritual fruitfulness. Effective leaders can inspire, guide, and support their members, fostering an environment where the word of God can take root and flourish.

1. Modeling Spiritual Practices: Leaders should model spiritual practices such as prayer, scripture study, worship, and service. By demonstrating a commitment to these disciplines, leaders can inspire members to follow their example and prioritize their spiritual growth.

2. Providing Vision and Direction: Effective leaders provide a clear vision and direction for the community, aligning its activities and initiatives with the teachings of the Bible. This vision can help members understand the purpose and goals of their faith journey and motivate them to engage fully in the life of the community.

3. Offering Pastoral Care and Support: Leaders should provide pastoral care and support to members, addressing their spiritual, emotional, and practical needs. This care can include counseling, prayer, visitation, and crisis

intervention. By offering compassionate and attentive support, leaders can help members navigate challenges and remain rooted in their faith.

4. Facilitating Opportunities for Growth: Leaders should create and facilitate opportunities for growth, such as Bible studies, workshops, retreats, and service projects. By providing a variety of avenues for engagement, leaders can meet the diverse needs and interests of their members, promoting a well-rounded and vibrant community.

5. Encouraging Collaboration and Participation: Leaders should encourage collaboration and participation within the community, fostering a sense of ownership and shared responsibility. This can include involving members in decision-making processes, seeking their input on initiatives, and empowering them to take on leadership roles.

6. Promoting Inclusivity and Diversity: Effective leaders promote inclusivity and diversity within the community, ensuring that all members feel valued and respected. This involves creating an environment where different perspectives, backgrounds, and experiences are welcomed and celebrated. Inclusivity fosters a richer and more dynamic community, reflecting the diversity of the body of Christ.

7. Fostering a Culture of Accountability: Leaders should foster a culture of accountability, where members are encouraged to hold each other accountable for their commitments and actions. This can include establishing accountability groups, providing regular check-ins, and encouraging transparency and honesty. Accountability helps members stay focused on their spiritual goals and maintain their commitment to growth.

8. Celebrating Achievements and Milestones: Leaders should celebrate the achievements and milestones of their members, recognizing their efforts and progress in their faith journey. This can include celebrating baptisms, confirmations, anniversaries, and other significant events. Celebrating these moments fosters a sense of community and encouragement, motivating members to continue their growth.

The Impact of a Receptive Community

A community that cultivates receptive hearts and promotes spiritual fruitfulness can have a profound impact on its members and the broader society. The following are some of the potential outcomes of a receptive community:

1. Strengthened Faith and Resilience: Members of a receptive community are likely to develop a stronger and more resilient faith. They are better equipped to navigate challenges, persevere through trials, and remain steadfast in their commitment to Christ. This resilience enables them to face life's uncertainties with confidence and hope.

2. Increased Spiritual Growth: A community that prioritizes spiritual growth and provides opportunities for engagement fosters continuous development among its members. Increased spiritual growth leads to a deeper understanding of God's word, a closer relationship with Him, and greater maturity in faith.

3. Enhanced Witness and Outreach: A receptive community serves as a powerful witness to the transformative power of the gospel. Its members' lives reflect the love, grace, and truth of Christ, drawing others to Him. Enhanced witness and outreach efforts can lead to more people encountering the gospel and experiencing its life-changing impact.

4. Stronger Relationships and Fellowship: A supportive and engaged community fosters strong relationships and fellowship among its members. These relationships provide mutual encouragement, support, and accountability, creating a sense of belonging and unity. Strong fellowship helps members feel connected and valued, promoting overall well-being.

5. Greater Impact on Society: A receptive community can have a significant impact on society through its service, advocacy, and outreach efforts. By addressing practical needs, promoting justice, and demonstrating compassion, the community can make a positive difference in the lives of individuals and contribute to the common good.

6. Fulfillment of God's Purposes: Ultimately, a receptive community fulfills God's purposes by living out the teachings of Christ and advancing His Kingdom. This fulfillment involves making disciples, promoting righteousness, and being a light in the world. A community that aligns with God's purposes experiences His blessings and favor.

Conclusion

The parable of the sower offers profound insights into the dynamics of spiritual receptivity and growth. By understanding the significance of each type of soil and the process of cultivating a receptive heart, believers can strive to be fruitful followers of Christ.

James 1:21 calls believers to "get rid of all moral filth and the evil that is so prevalent and humbly accept the word planted in you, which can save you." This verse encapsulates the essence of the parable's application, emphasizing the importance of removing hindrances and humbly receiving God's word.

By prioritizing regular engagement with scripture, developing a prayerful life, practicing spiritual disciplines, seeking community and accountability, embracing simplicity and contentment, trusting in God's provision, and embracing trials as opportunities for growth, believers can cultivate a productive and resilient faith.

The broader implications for discipleship, spiritual growth, and community life highlight the importance of fostering spiritual depth and resilience within the church. Effective leadership, practical steps for community engagement, and the impact of a receptive community can lead to strengthened faith, increased spiritual growth, enhanced witness and outreach, stronger relationships, and greater societal impact.

As we seek to grow in our faith and support others in their journey, let us strive to cultivate hearts that are receptive to God's word, able to bear fruit for the Kingdom of Heaven and make a lasting impact in the world. By doing so, we fulfill God's purposes and experience the abundant life that He promises.

Don't miss out!

Visit the website below and you can sign up to receive emails whenever Gregory Allen Parker publishes a new book. There's no charge and no obligation.

https://books2read.com/r/B-A-SLYZB-XSBKE

BOOKS 2 READ

Connecting independent readers to independent writers.

Did you love *The Parable of the Sower*? Then you should read *The Twelve Tribes*[1] by Gregory Allen Parker!

Explore the origins, trials, and triumphs of the Twelve Tribes of Israel through a detailed narrative enriched by key biblical verses. From God's promise to Abraham, the birth of Jacob's sons, and Joseph's rise in Egypt, to the Exodus, the Giving of the Law, and the conquest of Canaan, each chapter unveils pivotal moments in Israel's history. Witness the establishment and fall of the united kingdom, the exile, and the eventual return and restoration, all underscored by themes of faith, resilience, and divine promise. This comprehensive outline provides a spiritual and historical journey through the Bible's most profound events.

---

1. https://books2read.com/u/31ddJa

2. https://books2read.com/u/31ddJa

About the Author

Pastor Gregory Allen Parker, a graduate of Trinity Theological Seminary, is a devoted pastor and acclaimed author of Christian fiction. With over two decades of ministry experience, his books explore faith's challenges and triumphs, offering readers inspiring and spiritually rich narratives. Celebrated for his compassionate pastoral care and insightful sermons, Pastor Parker's storytelling reflects his deep understanding of Christian values. When not writing or preaching, he enjoys family time, community volunteering, and the outdoors, continuing to inspire and uplift through his faith and craft.